OCULUM

OCULUM

BY PHILIPPA
DOWDING

DCB

Canada Council **Conseil des Arts**
for the Arts **du Canada**

 ONTARIO ARTS COUNCIL
CONSEIL DES ARTS DE L'ONTARIO
an Ontario government agency
un organisme du gouvernement de l'Ontario

 Canadian   Patrimoine
Heritage   canadien   **Canadä**

The publisher gratefully acknowledges the support of the Canada Council for the Arts
and the Ontario Arts Council for its publishing program. We acknowledge the financial
support of the Government of Canada through the Canada Book Fund (CBF) for
our publishing activities, and the Government of Ontario through the Ontario Media
Development Corporation, an agency of the Ontario Ministry of Culture, and the
Ontario Book Publishing Tax Credit Program.

LIBRARY AND ARCHIVES CANADA CATALOGUING IN PUBLICATION

Library and Archives Canada Cataloguing in Publication

Dowding, Philippa, 1963-, author
Oculum / Philippa Dowding.

Issued in print and electronic formats.
ISBN 978-1-77086-512-9 (softcover). — ISBN 978-1-77086-513-6 (HTML)

I. Title.

PS8607.O9874O28 2018   jC813'.6   C2018-900879-2
C2018-900880-6

United States Library of Congress Control Number: 2017964198

Cover: Emma Dolan
Interior text design: Tannice Goddard, bookstopress.com

Printed and bound in Canada.

Manufactured by Friesens in Altona, Manitoba, Canada in March, 2018.

This book is printed on 100% post-consumer waste recycled paper.

DCB
An imprint of Cormorant Books Inc.
10 St. Mary Street, Suite 615, Toronto, Ontario, M4Y 1P9
www.dancingcatbooks.com
www.cormorantbooks.com

For Sarah,
and her many boys.

Oculum (noun): Latin for eye; in architecture, a circular *oculus* allows light through the top of the Roman Pantheon and similar ancient domed structures. Oculum aperui: I opened an eye.

We have left you,
The thousand chosen,
Kept you all safe here, at the fall.
There is a door,
And you must find it,
There is a door, within the wall.
Be the brave ones,
Then pass beyond it,
The Mothers shall rise, at the call.
      — For the Children of Oculum

MIRANDA1

"Mother?"

"Yes, Miranda my darling?"

Mother says this as she tucks me deeply under my covers.

"Mother, have you seen the Seed Park today?"

Mother hums a bit as she tidies the room and then comes back to my bed. She tilts her head, which always looks so sweet. I wonder where she learned that behavior. The worn leather at her neck creaks, the metal at her jaw squeaks softly.

"No. What is happening in the Seed Park?"

I am so excited, I can barely tell her. But I keep my voice calm. As Miranda1, I cannot be too excitable.

"Buds! Everywhere! The fruit trees are about to return to us, Mother. It has been a long wait."

Mother nods and brings her face close to mine. I love the scent of her machine oil. It is so calming, so motherly. She whispers, "Regulus has told me a secret."

Mother almost never whispers, because it seems difficult for her, but she does, in a raspy, coughy way. There is no one else here. I can't imagine why she feels the need.

"What? What did he tell you?" If she could smile, Mother would be smiling now.

"Oculum will be opened tomorrow."

I gasp and sit up, undoing the carefully tucked blanket.

"Really? I have to tell William1!"

Mother whirrs and tucks me back into my bed.

"William1 already knows," she soothes. "Now go to sleep." She holds me briefly in her cool, metallic arms, and I feel calmer. She does give good hugs, along with the excellent blanket tucking.

"Goodnight, Mother," I whisper.

"Goodnight, Miranda my darling," she whispers back. The silver "M1" on her purple armband glistens in the low light of the room, a perfect match to my own armband. Mother blows out the candles, then I hear her leave and roll along to her cupboard. I have fallen asleep to the gentle squeak of her wheels as she exits my bedroom since I was four. It makes me drowsy. Tonight, though, I notice that her wheels are very squeaky again. I shall have to tell Toolman.

I fall asleep and dream about Mother's metallic grip, the opening of Oculum tomorrow, and the promise of fresh air.

The next morning, Mother wakes me with a gentle shake. I sit and draw my knees up as she opens the curtains. It's gloomy outside.

"Will Regulus open Oculum today?" I ask sleepily. "It looks dark out." Mother shakes her head, which is creaky. She really does need a visit to Toolman. I shall have to broach it with her, which is tricky. She hates to be reminded that she is getting older.

"No."

"Why?"

Mother stops at the window and looks out at the quiet streets, the spotless marble sidewalks, the pristine row of houses with their color-coded doors. In the distance is the Seed Park, and beyond that, at the edge of my vision, is the great wall of Oculum. All is quiet, gently calm, Oculum dwellers are being woken by their Mothers, just as I am.

But there is a note to Mother's voice that is upsetting.

"Why not, Mother?" I ask again.

She turns to look at me, and those whirring, almost-human eyes register concern. Or what I know to be her concerned look.

"A Black Rain is on its way." I frown and get out of bed. Mother starts to dress me in my favorite long, dark frock. She buttons me up the back and I slip into my shoes.

"We have not had a Black Rain in a long while." I say this simply, and we look at each other. She tilts her head again.

"And yet Regulus says it is so. Oculum stays closed. Now you must hurry. Your Correction Day." She nods at the door and fusses and whirrs about the room, tidying and straightening. When she is finished, I hear her roll back into her closet and shut the door.

There is a bowl of fruit downstairs beside the front door, and I take a peach. The flesh is sweet and soft and smells delicious. The Seed Park grows lovely, long-lasting fruit. This is from last year, stored and dried safely in our dark, cool pantry.

Mother is right — today is a Correction Day. I hate this part of my duties, but someone must correct the misdeeds of the younger children. We Mirandas must do our best. I walk along the sidewalk, say hello to the other children as I meet them, then stop at the quiet, musty Punishment Hall. It is thankfully little-used and empty most of the time. I pick up my assignment inside the door and read it over.

A Jake. So an eleven-year-old. This is Jake47, a smart, rambunctious boy. The assignment sheet says, "Obstinate refusal to follow rules. Touched the Will-Book. PUNISHMENT: ONE SLAP." I read it over again. A *slap*? With my hand?

This is new for me. Usually, it's a stern scolding or the setting of extra chores. Or I have to accompany a particularly unruly child to talk to Regulus in the Oculum Senate. I've never had to strike anyone before. Regulus must be very cross with this child. I look around briefly, wondering if there's been a mistake. But I know it's not a mistake. Regulus doesn't make mistakes.

I step lightly into the hall. Jake47 sits on his hands in the chair at the center of the room and looks up at me. He's sweet, but he is nervous. His green armband has a silver "J" and the number "47" on it. The hall has only his chair and nowhere for me to sit. I suppose this is to make me seem imposing. I tower over him.

"Good morning, Jake47." I try to use their full names; it also makes me seem more grown up.

"Good morning, Miranda1." He shoots a quick look at my own armband: purple for Miranda, with a silver "M1" on it.

"Do you know why you are here?"

He nods. "I touched the WillBook," he says quietly. I nod too and *hmmm* a little. How exactly, and when, am I supposed to slap him?

"I see. And why did you touch what was forbidden?" And where do I slap him? His arm? His face?

"We … we were talking about seeds in Teaching Hall. How seeds are for everyone." Jake47 looks up at me, and I can see he is afraid but also confused.

"Yes, that's correct. Wasn't Teacher clear on that? The words are simple. We all learn them: 'We have given you every plant seed, and every tree which has fruit; it will be food for you.'" I'm puzzled. These are the very first words that we learn in our lessons. Our Teacher drills this into us. Seeds are life. Seeds are for everyone. What can Jake47 possibly not understand about seeds? He looks down at his feet, which swing back and forth.

He's short and the chair is a tall one.

"Then Teacher said that the WillBook is the seed of all thought, but it doesn't seem the same, so I touched it, to see." He looks up at me. "It's just that I don't think seeds ARE for everyone. The Fandoms in the Outside don't have them ..."

"STOP!" I shout this, more in surprise than anything else. It's not the first time a younger child has mentioned the Fandoms. Or the Outside. I heard the whisperings too when I was his age. But it is not allowed to speak of such things, and the sooner he realizes it, the better. The shadowy, frightening images of faces and eyes that flare and dance against the opaque wall of Oculum from time to time are Fandoms. Flickers of light, but not alive. Brief reflections of sky, nothing more.

I use my best stern, scolding voice and draw up to my full height, which is quite tall.

"That is nonsense, Jake47. You know it. There are NO SUCH THINGS as Fandoms. There is no such thing as Outside. The seeds are for all of us. All of Oculum. I had a peach this morning. Your Mother must have put out a peach for you today as well. The fruit trees are budding in the Seed Park right now."

The boy nods at me, and he stops swinging his legs. "Yes, Miranda1. I did have a peach this morning." I tilt my head a little then stop, realizing I must look just like Mother.

"Do you promise not to touch the WillBook again?" Jake47 nods.

"Do you also promise not to listen to the pointless whispers of other children? No more talk of Fandoms and Outside?" He nods again.

"Do not forget my words. Go to your next activity then, Jake47." I walk over to him and playfully, gently slap his shoulder.

"And be a good boy," I add, watching him leap out of his chair and dash out the door. He doesn't even look back — he's gone. Off to Teaching Hall, or chores, or a scheduled play event.

The assignment sheet didn't say how *forceful* a slap to give. A gentle one seemed appropriate for a young boy just listening to rumors. I did my duty.

I step outside into the gloomy day. The air is hot, unclean. The promise of fresh air gone, I'm even more aware of the oppressive atmosphere, but I can do nothing about it.

I turn toward the Seed Park, where I have a meeting with William1.

It is a short walk, and no one waves or talks to me, but I feel heavy and tired when I arrive. William1 waits for me beside the pond.

The lights are on in the firmament high above, and they shine on the Seed Park, warming the air. Since the fruit trees are beginning to bud, the lights are kept on longer than usual. The great fans run near the Seed Park, cleaning the air.

The Seed Park is warm and has fresher air than anywhere else, especially when Oculum has been closed for so long. It's the main reason why I enjoy it. It's also beautiful and peaceful, with all the growing trees and fruits and some flowers. There are worker bees droning, and Treekeepers prune, tend, and quietly work among the trees. Small greenhouses dot the grounds where we grow greens and vegetables. One greenhouse is full of new cuts from the fruit trees, another is full of seeds. We all have lessons in the Seed Park every week on how to tend fruit trees, how to prune, and how to pick ripe fruit, how to plant and grow. We are even learning how to tend bees, since another hive has just been awakened.

The pond is at the center of the park, and when I come upon him, William1 is deep in thought. There are a few other Mirandas and Williams nearby, and I greet each one politely. They smile and go back to their talk. Whenever I am with William1, no one approaches us. I suppose we may be intimidating as the oldest children of Oculum.

He clasps my arm in the regular greeting, his red armband with the silver "W1" upon it brushing my own purple armband. But there is something wrong, I can tell immediately.

"William1, I am pleased to see you," I say, straightening my frock. He leads me to one of the long benches, away from the others. The fountain in the middle of the pond gently sprays water toward the distant lights and makes a cheerful, pleasant splashing.

"Miranda1, I am pleased to see you," he says in return, but he has a strange look on his face. I have known William1 all my life. We were awoken just days apart. I know his every look. "How was your Correction Day?" he asks, distracted.

"Oh, that was a Jake. Jake47. He was just inquisitive, lacking in impulse control. He touched the WillBook. He had questions about Seeds. Nothing serious." I don't mention the slap or the odd request from Regulus to administer it.

"Honestly, he seemed so frightened and small, I don't think he'll do it again. He was listening to rumors that children tell. About Fandoms. Outside. That kind of thing." William1 hasn't really been listening, but when I say *Fandoms*, he sits up straighter.

"William, are you all right?" He takes a sudden deep breath. He looks around at the others talking quietly by the pond or along the paths beneath the trees. As the oldest, Mirandas and Williams are allowed the most time in the Seed Park, one hour each day. The younger children, an eleven-year-old Jake or Jane for instance, would only be allowed one hour a week in the park, and none if they had misbehaved. Jake47 won't be visiting this week, I'm sure.

It is a privilege to be here, whether we are working or taking our leisure.

William1 draws close to me and whispers, "I have found something. I must show someone, and you are the only person I can trust." He speaks so quietly, I can barely hear him.

"Will you walk with me?" he whispers again.

I nod. I can't for the life of me imagine what William1 could have found or what is making him so nervous. We never need to whisper. We leave the bench, and a few Mirandas sit down in our place, joined a moment later by a William, William32. They laugh and chat. They're the same age as William1 and I, all awoken sometime after us in the same year, but suddenly I feel very far away from them.

I don't like the look on William1's face at all.

He quietly steers me along a path that leads to the great curved wall of Oculum. We can't get too close of course; it is forbidden. There is a well-marked fence that we are not allowed to cross, and there are Sentries to enforce the rules. No one is allowed to touch the walls that ring the world. The vast, opaque walls arch to the firmament and touch far above our heads. They are the edge of everything.

But why would we want to go near the wall anyway? I cannot understand why William is drawing us so near.

The Seed Park is large, though, and soon we are out of sight of anyone else. There are no Treekeepers working near this part of the park. We're all alone. The forbidden wall is not far from us, and I realize as William draws me along that I have never been this close to it. The enormous filter fans work away, taking tired air out, drawing fresh air in. A gentle breeze stirs the leaves at this end of the park, stirs my hair, the hem of my frock. The noise of the fans is like a gentle breath, in and out.

William leads me to a large rosebush growing up a trellis, where he looks around, then draws me behind the trellis. It is forbidden to do this. Mother always tells me so. Teacher tells us. Regulus tells us.

We must not hide alone together. Especially not the Williams and Mirandas. We are the oldest. We must set an example for the younger children.

"What ..." I begin, but William shakes his head. His eyes tell me to be silent, then he looks over my shoulder, and I see a Sentry. It's far away, at the edge of the park, but close enough to catch us if it sees us. It rolls slowly along the curved wall then turns and rolls the other way. It will be back.

I can't imagine why William would endanger us in this way.

William looks over his shoulder. The massive Oculum Arm that stretches from the ground floor of the Oculum Senate to the top of our world looks almost small from here. But William is not looking at the Arm. I follow his gaze toward the wall and catch my breath. I clamp my lips together, since it would not do to gasp out loud.

There is something I have never seen before, clearly cut into the wall. William has found something that is forbidden, unthinkable. Something that by its very nature must open and close.

There is a shape, a rectangle. A heavy vine grows near the shape, up and over and along, partly obscuring it.

But there is no mistaking what he is showing me.

William1 has found a door.

We look at each other, and I can barely breathe.

There is a *door* in the wall of our world.

MANNFRED

Cranker holds his arm above the Littlun's head. The Littlun snivels and whines and jumps up and down, trying to grab the bread that Cranker holds high.

"I took it, Cranker! Give it back!" Cranker considers this. He sniffs the bread, licks it, smiles down at the boy.

"You took it? *You*? Where from?"

The boy hangs his head. He points at a group of even smaller Littluns throwing stones at a stray, one-eyed dog across the footbridge.

"Grannie give it to them."

Cranker tried taking shots at this dog last week, but it slunk off soon as it saw the slingshot. The dog barks, wags its tail, hopeful, but stays across the river out of range of the Littluns. And Cranker's slingshot.

Stupidest dog I ever saw, though. Why's it back here? We got nothing to give it.

"What's the law?" Cranker says, patient. If I could count how many times Cranker says this to the Littluns every day, I'd be a genius. There's not a number that high.

"Cranker gets it first," the boy mumbles. He stopped

crying, but there are perfect tear-tracks down his thin cheeks.

Cranker nods. "Yes, Cranker gets it first." He takes a wide open bite of the bread then breaks off a piece and hands it to me.

"And who gets it second?" The boy shoots me an angry look but points at me and says, "Him. Mann." I put the piece of bread in my mouth and start chewing. It's hard and dry, and it does take the edge off the hole in my stomach, but it's never enough.

"Very good. And what else?" The boy has bright blue eyes and shoots a look at Cranker that says, *You won't always be the toughest.*

Cranker repeats his question, patient and calm. "What *else?*" The boy toes the muck at his feet with a busted shoe too big for him.

"Don't tell Grannie."

"Good!" Cranker breaks off a small piece of the bread and hands it to the Littlun, who tears off with it, behind the midden, past the henhouse and to the back of Grannie's house. He disappears into the landscape, since he's made of the same stuff: filth and muck.

Cranker and me watch the other Littluns chase the dog away, then they start to romp in the black water of the slimy river. The biggest Littlun holds the smallest Littlun underwater and makes the others laugh. This is what we did at their age. Stab each other with sticks, throw rocks, hold smaller heads under water, and bury each other in muck. Once in a while, though, it goes too far, and we lose a Littlun. We got a cemetery in back of the village with flags marking each stony grave. Illness, accidents, disease. We seen it all.

I walk over and shout at them, and they run off. I finish my bread, and Cranker passes me the second last piece. He pops the last piece into his mouth.

"The Shiny Man is coming."

I shake my head. I'm a lot bigger than Cranker, 'though I'm a year or two younger. I look down into his dirty face, his hair standing stiff and unwashed all around his head. It's about time Grannie made us all take our springtime bath.

"You lie." I can get away with this. I'm Cranker's best friend, his only friend, too.

"No, Grannie told the neighbor. I was chasing a FatRat, and I heard her." I look around the tiny, mostly empty village. We live on a tree-covered island surrounded by the slimy black river. The only way to get to our ten broken-down houses is over the footbridge. We aren't what you'd call an important stop on the road to the City.

I almost can't remember the last time the Shiny Man came here.

Grannie comes out on her porch and rings the bell for soup. Cranker and me didn't catch any FatRats today, so there's no fresh roasted meat. But the chicken broth soup will have carrot and runner beans from Grannie's greenhouse. And it'll be warm, which is something. We'll have milk from one of Grannie's goats.

I follow Cranker and the Littluns into the house and sit at the huge table. I grab a wooden bowl, and Grannie slops warm soup into it. There's bread on our trenchers, one thin slice each. When all the bowls are full, we bow our heads and Grannie says what she says over every meal: "May the sun shine, the sweet rain fall, and the fruit trees blossom once again." Then she mumbles under her breath, "What I wouldn't give for a peach."

The Littluns fall to it, eating and slurping until every crumb, every taste, is gone.

Cranker and me sit at the edge of the table, eating in silence. I got no idea what a peach is, or an apple, or a pear, or the other things Grannie calls fruit, because they all vanished long ago.

But I do know what the Shiny Man is. It would be something to see the Shiny Man again. Most of the Littluns at the table weren't even born the last time he visited.

More than likely, though, Cranker is lying.

But soon enough it's clear that Cranker didn't lie.

The Shiny Man DID come. We all waited on Grannie's porch, watching the footbridge, for two days. Then one of the Littluns came tearing across the river, calling and singing about the Shiny Man.

Then there he was.

He was pretty much as I remembered him, tall, mounted on a great horse pulling the Shiny wagon, dressed in a shining shirt and shining pants, with huge shining boots. He wore a tall, bright helmet with a white feather waving high above. He had a big, red beard hanging down to his chest and a powerful build, with arms that bulged with muscle. He was quite a sight.

His horse was huge, much bigger than our old nags Nancy and Nellie, and it pulled the wagon behind it. The wagon rode low to the ground and had four doors with busted glass windows and seats inside it. There was a wheel for steering tied to the Shiny Man's horse. The wagon sat upon four rubber wheels, which we don't see often. We only got wooden wheels on our carts.

But the Shiny Man isn't like us. He's like a memory of a past time, the Olden Begones, as Grannie calls them. She tells us stories sometimes, and in the Olden Begones, the wagons drove magically along without horses. Later, when she asked him, the Shiny Man opened the front lid of the wagon and showed us what he called an "engine" inside, the part that once upon a time made the wagon run without horses. But I don't see how that could be true.

The Shiny Man travels from village to village with his goods. He gets them from the City, from other Grannies in other villages, even from faraway places, and then brings them to us and places like ours, in the lonely villages where people still are.

We need shiny goods made of metal, too, just like everyone else.

He spreads what Grannie calls "his wares" around the countryside, far and wide, and he gets wares in return from the people he visits. Maybe sweaters knit by a Grannie, or hens, or a precious goat, to carry with him and share with others in the next village. Every village gives him something in return for his shiny goods, and on it goes.

He crosses the river and draws his horse and wagon into the muddy track in the center of our ten houses, and all the Littluns, Cranker, me, the two neighbors, and Grannie go to greet him. He looks like a hero standing among all us filthy beings. I never seen so many teeth beaming in mud-covered faces.

"Hello!" the Shiny Man calls through his helmet, and all the Littluns call hello back. They crowd around him and want to touch his horse. I touch the horse, too, and wonder at his muscle and soft nose. It's a huge dray horse, good for pulling and plowing. Then we all draw close around the wagon and peer through the broken windows at the treasure inside.

I'm amazed by what I see.

The wagon is filled with all the shiny goods we could ever need. New pots and pans for Grannie. Metal wheels for our handcarts. A metal box with a lid on it for safe storage. Metal tools, like a hammer and a screwdriver and a small handsaw. All of ours are wore out or broke, so we need them. There are toys for the Littluns that look just like the Shiny Man's wagon but fit in a hand. He gives these out, and the Littluns run off down the street to watch over their treasure and to fight each other for them.

There are new knives for skinning FatRats and cutting carrots and beans. There are bows and arrows and a machine called a crossbow, which looks vicious but efficient. Cranker eyes them, but the Shiny Man says they're for another village. There's a new slingshot for Cranker, though, with a strong rubber spring, which is good because his old one is almost wore out, too.

And then there's something for me I never had before: a knife with a leather sheath.

When Grannie asks the Shiny Man to show us knives for two boys such as us, I almost fall over. When the Shiny Man hands me my own knife, my first one, he smiles and says, "Use it well, Mannfred. You're a good boy, a strong and honest boy. You're nearly thirteen now, almost a man. Let this knife be your sword." Then he pats my back, and I feel strange.

No one gave me a knife before, and no one calls me by my full name. Not since I can remember. Not Cranker, not even Grannie.

I'm Mann.

The Shiny Man hands us bags of oats and grain for bread, barley for soup, some salt for preserving goat meat. There are blankets and blue flannel cloth too, and

Grannie gets a bunch of both. And needles and thread, which is also good because our clothes, such as they are, are nothing more than rags. And a fine new pair of scissors, which is fascinating to me. Grannie always keeps her scissors hid, and they're so old they're held together with wire. A new pair is a huge gift for her. She looks almost young with the excitement of all these treasures. Her gray hair is all over, and her apron is full of brand new shiny metal tools. Cranker and me stand and stare at the wonder of it.

Then Grannie hands the Shiny Man two big bundles of clean, mended clothes the Littluns all outgrown but are still good for someone else in some other village. She hands over a bundle of sweaters and socks she knit from wool she saved for this very thing. She also hands the Shiny Man a basket of fresh hen's eggs and a sack of carrots and beans.

The Shiny Man takes all Grannie's gifts and stacks them at the back of the wagon. There's a lot of sacks back there. Every village he passes through, he takes and he receives.

But then there was the biggest surprise of all.

After he puts everything away, and the job of swapping his shiny wares for our goods is over, the Shiny Man reaches into a special covered seat and brings out the biggest surprise yet: a *baby!*

A new Littlun!

We haven't had a baby here in a long time; no one has

dropped one at the footbridge or knocked on the door and run in the dead of night, the usual way of getting Littluns. It's a girl, also something we haven't ever had. Right now all the Littluns are boys. The baby girl has soft, curly hair and huge brown eyes. She wakes and smiles at us all.

Grannie calls her Lisle, wraps her up tight in a bright blue sling around her shoulder, and sticks a rag soaked in goat's milk in Lisle's little mouth. I can tell by Grannie's soft voice and bright eyes that she's happy with the baby. She thanks the Shiny Man, and he seems happy too. He doesn't bring many people new babies, he says. And never girls.

The Shiny Man shows us coins, too, which I seen before but which don't mean much. They're just silver and gold and there's no use for them, but the Shiny Man tells us that in the Olden Begones, people gave the shiny coins for food and such. He hands them out to us to keep in our pockets as something to remember his visit by. I never had a coin before, either.

Then when the Littluns are gone to sleep, he takes off his shiny suit and helmet. He's just a man under all that metal, a big man with a red beard. He takes Grannie, me, and Cranker outside and shows us another thing I never seen before, only heard of: a gun.

They're so rare, most people never seen one. Cranker asks him where he got it. It's a holdover from the Olden Begones, he says, and no one can make them now.

He let Grannie hold it, and Cranker, then me. It was heavy in my hand. It felt alive somehow, like something mysterious. He showed us a box of what he called "ammunition" and how the bullets fit perfect in the gun.

Then he pointed it at a far-off tree and showed us how to take aim.

Then he fired it.

Cranker had the biggest smile I ever seen, but me? I was just scared. What a horrible loud noise.

Then he sent me and Cranker off to find FatRats for a late meal, and he and Grannie sat talking by the fire for the rest of the night. But it was all dull adult talk, the little that I heard through the doors to the room we all sleep in, about food, crops, and what was happening in the City these days.

The Shiny Man left the next day.

And as soon as he did, the Black Rain comes.

For two days, the Black Rain comes in greasy sheets that fall from the sky like oily soup. It slides down the roof and off the trees. It hits the ground harder than normal rain and smells different. I can't name like what, though. Grannie says "brimstone," whatever that might be.

It's a long rain. It comes now and then, but lately we seen less and less of it. When I was little, the Black Rain came twice a year or even three times, but this is the first rain like it in a long while.

This is the hardest rain I ever seen, though.

The rain comes straight down in sheets and hisses where it lands. Big trees can live, small, delicate things can't. Grannie tells us this is why there's almost no grass, just tough bushes and not much else but mud all around us. I think about that sometimes, how I never known much but mud, but once there was green grass here, long ago. There's tall grass and grains out in the fields, but it's not green and never was.

When the Black Rain starts, me and Cranker help Grannie get all the herbs and potted plants into the greenhouse. We strap heavy oilcloth over the henhouse and find all the wandering goats in the woods and put them in their pen behind the midden. We tie down the door and make sure none of the rain can get in.

Then we help her cut up an old sheet in strips and get the masks over the howling faces of the Littluns, but that was a bust. By end of the first day of Black Rain, the Littluns are bored and whiny and don't want to stay indoors anymore.

Already most of them ripped off their masks and hid them where Grannie can't see. Cranker and me sit on the porch with Grannie's masks tied tight over our mouth and nose like she told us. We got some sense, at least.

So the Littluns are all indoors, whacking each other and brawling and whining. Grannie has some of them quieted, though, and is showing them letters and numbers. She's got one book she had since she was little, by a man called Aesop, with pictures in it that are a wonder. I can hear she starts reading the story of *The Fox and the Crow*, and the Littluns all stop their yowling to listen, although they heard it a thousand times by now.

I can read. Grannie taught me enough to read Aesop's stories, anyway. But the truth is, I already knew how to read a little and do numbers, too, when I came to Grannie, even though I was such a Littlun. I have no memory of the time before her, but there was one. My different way of speaking comes from then, some of my words.

But we all got a time before Grannie.

Cranker and me sit on the porch in Grannie's two old rockers. The porch is deep and covered, and we can hear and see the rain, but it can't touch us. Cranker looks weird, just his eyes and crazy, mud-stiff hair sticking out above his mask, and I must look strange, too. I'm using my new knife to work at a piece of wood. Grannie says Lisle needs something called a "soother" to suck on, so I'm making a shape that Grannie drew for me. A big round end with a little ring handle and a smaller bulb end.

When it's finished, Lisle will keep it in her mouth. It'll make her happy. I have to make it smooth and safe for her, and I like the idea of it, and working with my new knife.

Cranker has a big pile of pebbles beside his rocking chair, and he fires them from his slingshot at broken tin plates he nailed to trees before the rain. Every once in a while I hear a *plink-pock* as he hits one.

The one-eyed dog slinks into view by the footbridge. Cranker stops shooting at the trees, takes aim at the dog, but I make him stop.

"Don't," I say. Cranker pulls his hand away and scowls at me. At least I think it's a scowl. It's hard to tell with the mask on his face.

"Shove off, Manny Mann!" he says, all muffled through the cloth. He knows I hate the name Manny Mann. He's teasing me, challenging me.

The dog has his nose up and his thin tail down between his legs. His one good eye spies us, and he wags his tail, just the end. It near breaks my heart. Stupidest dog I ever saw.

"Get!" I yell. I stand up and wave my arms. I hope to scare it off, since Cranker is a dead shot. He stands and takes aim at the dog, a perfect killer. I could fight him, I could stop him. I'm bigger. He draws the strong new slingshot with all his strength, straight along his jawline to the ear.

Just as Cranker lets fly, I jump up and push his arm. The rock flies wild, and the dog runs off.

"Festering gobs, Manny!" Cranker turns on me, his temper flaring. It's why Grannie named him Cranker when he was little; he's quick to burn, ready for a fight. He wants to hit me, but we stopped fighting a few years ago. I always win.

He narrows his eyes above the mask and hisses at me. "He's going to die, anyway. You know it. I was doing him a favor."

He's right. The dog could die, like most of the others.

"He's not dead yet," I say through the thick mask. "Who says you get to decide?"

Then I turn and stomp into the house.

MIRANDA1

It is a Black Rain today.

Oculum is closed, as the greasy, dark waters flow down in heavy streams. We are used to the sound of the regular rains as they fall on Oculum. It's a peaceful drumming sound. But the Black Rain is different. It's heavy, oily, and thick. It slides, and sticks, and slides again. Thankfully, it has become less common. Black Rains used to be frequent, two or three times a year, but this is the first one in a long while.

Oculum is a dark place today.

William1 and I are standing in front of Regulus, who looks down at us from his mighty seat. We are in the Oculum Senate, the great marble hall of order and quiet. Regulus is our leader, taller than the Mothers, even taller than the Sentries. He makes sure that Oculum runs smoothly, that all the children and helpers are cared for and happy, that trees grow, that food is in good supply.

He's also the only one among the Sentries, Mothers, and other helpers who is *not* on wheels. Regulus has two legs, two feet, two arms, and deft, mechanical hands. He is made of leather and metal like the others, but he's different. His face holds emotion, his sensible eyes surprise you.

The great Oculum Arm sits behind him. I have stood here with William1 once a week since I turned twelve, yet I am still impressed. The Arm is a mighty machine, a marvel, held to the floor with bolts as tall as William, an enormous corkscrew that disappears straight up into the heights of Oculum, to the firmament. If I were to tilt my head back and peer upward, I would see the Arm in the distance, touching the top of Oculum. One day, I would like to be here when Regulus sets the machine in motion (however that it is done) and watch as it opens the top of our world to the sun and the breeze.

I have seen the Arm working from afar, of course, but never from this room.

Regulus peers down at us, and I try not to look afraid.

William1 and I have helped him decide punishments, schooling, chores, and exercise schedules for the one thousand souls of Oculum, feeding arrangements, housing, timing of fruit growth, and much more.

It was my idea, in fact, to color-code the front doors of the houses to match our armbands. My front door is purple, the color for Mirandas. My door has my number, a large, silver "M1" on it. In the same way, William1's front door is dark red, the color for all Williams, and his has "W1" upon it. We all have a color and a number, on our arms, on our doors. It's a simple and effective way to identify each other.

I have never been exactly comfortable standing in front of Regulus, but today my hands are clammy and my heart is beating too quickly. I am nervous. I have never had a secret to keep from Regulus before.

William and I have not spoken since we saw the door in the Seed Park. We walked away from the rosebush trellis separately three days ago, and we haven't sought each other out since. I haven't been able to sleep nor concentrate in lessons. Teacher was very cross with me yesterday when I could not remember the correct meaning for "stamen." Mother has asked me repeatedly what is wrong, but I simply cannot tell her. I can't believe it myself and can think of no way to explain it.

Why would there be a *door* in the wall of Oculum?

I cannot fathom it.

It must open, it must close. This is the nature of doors. But what does it open upon? What does it close upon? Who would ever open it and walk through? And what would you walk through into? More Oculum? Or something else?

What would be awaiting you on the other side? The very thought makes me shudder. I can tell that William is also plagued. He has dark circles under his eyes, and he looks like he hasn't slept since we last spoke.

Regulus has just asked me a question, and I have to ask him to repeat it. He lifts a creaky silver eyebrow and shifts upon his mighty chair.

"I asked you to please explain why you and William1

were hiding in the Seed Park?"

I should have paid attention! I shouldn't have been thinking about the door! What else has been said? William steps in.

"We were not hiding, Regulus," he says calmly.

"The Sentry says that you were," Regulus says. A Sentry waits beside him. It must be the same one from a few days ago, but I didn't think it saw us. And it's impossible to tell one from another, since they are all the same: tall, broad, on wheels, and not very bright.

William shakes his head and smiles at Regulus. "No, Regulus. We were not hiding. We were seeking a quiet place to be alone." William knows this is forbidden. I look at him sideways and try not to look surprised. What is he doing? Surely he is not about to mention the existence of the door? And Regulus would already know of it. He knows of everything.

"Then please explain." Regulus folds his metal fingers across his thin leather lap.

William moves closer to me and places his hand in mine.

"We are in love."

I am too shocked to hide it this time. I look at William quickly then look at the floor. He doesn't let go of my hand. I hear Regulus creak to his feet high above us and slowly descend the stairs until he stands directly in front of us. His long cape flaps with a sigh upon each stair behind him.

When he arrives in front of me, I stare at his metal toes. They are beautiful toes, carefully crafted and flexed. Regulus clears his throat and gently lifts my chin with his cool, metal fingers.

"Is this true?" he asks softly. "Is Miranda1 in love with her William?"

I cannot look away from the spinning, strangely mesmerizing eyes. Regulus gives off a gentle scent of machine oil, like Mother. I focus, take a breath, feel William1's warm hand in mine. I cannot imagine what game William is playing, but I trust him. I always have. I have known him since we were awoken in the nursery almost fourteen years ago, and I have never known him to lie or to lead me astray.

"Yes," I say simply. "Yes, we are in love."

Speaking the words makes me dizzy. Along with hiding, we are expressly forbidden to speak of love. We do not speak of it, we do not think of it, it does not exist.

I do not even know what it means. Not really. Only that it is forbidden.

Regulus takes a step away from us. He summons another Sentry and whispers to it. The Sentry wheels away quickly. Regulus turns back to us and sighs. He is quite theatrical when he wants to be.

"You know, of course, that hiding is forbidden. You also know that speaking of love is forbidden." William nods beside me, and I nod as well. What else am I to do? My eyes slowly take in the room. The Oculum Senate, the seat of power in our world.

My eyes glide over to the Seed Vault. Against the walls are shelf after shelf of precious seeds, locked in their sealed drawers, labeled and pictured. In idle moments of standing and listening to Regulus, I have counted as high as 816 drawers. But there are more, one thousand drawers in fact, and each drawer is filled with seeds for a different vegetable, plant, or tree.

Regulus is talking again. "We realize that you are getting older," he says. "But as the oldest, I must say that I am disappointed in you." He pauses for effect. In the silence, I hear the Black Rain slide down the dome, high above us.

"What am I to do with you?"

William is about to speak when two Mothers enter the room with a Sentry, one with a purple "M1" on her arm, the other with a red "W1." Our Mothers. My Mother wheels to my side and looks concerned. William1's Mother takes her place beside her charge.

Regulus turns to Mother. "Mother of Miranda1, did you know that your charge loves this William?"

Mother takes a sharp breath and looks at me. She cannot know what is going on, but she is wise, and she knows me well.

"Miranda1 has been acting strangely. I cannot say why." She moves a little closer, and I feel a bit calmer. She is protecting me, concerned.

Regulus turns to William's Mother.

"And you, Mother of William1. Have you noticed any odd behavior in your charge? Is he acting strangely as well?" Regulus pauses, then rasps in an almost-whisper, "Do you think he could be in *love*?" William's Mother is the oldest Mother, very wise and well-mannered. I have always liked her. She makes the odd, whirring sound of concern that Mothers make, but she looks evenly at Regulus.

"I do not know, Regulus, for I am not him. It could be normal for Williams and Mirandas. Especially the oldest."

Regulus strokes his leather beard, and stares down at the four of us. "I will hear no more of this love. Mother of Miranda1 and Mother of William1, I expressly *forbid* close contact between your charges. They may continue classes and chores together until I rearrange their schedule, but there is to be no more hiding. No more talk of *love*. Do you understand?"

Our Mothers both nod, but they look stricken. Regulus turns to William and me.

"William1, Miranda1. If I hear that you are alone together again, you will be punished. And it won't be a gentle slap, like you administered to Jake47, Miranda1. Yes, a Sentry told me about that." I didn't know a Sentry was watching in the Punishment Hall that day. Regulus pauses for effect as I take this in.

"If you are found hiding alone together again, one of you will be *banished*."

The word hangs before us. Both Mothers take a sharp breath. The Mother who raised me, who has watched over me since the day I entered her house as a four-year-old, lets out a tiny gasp. No one has ever been banished. Up until this very second, I didn't even know it was real or what it means, not really. I understand the word, of course: banishment means to be sent away. But sent away to ... where? A special, lonely house of Oculum that we don't know about yet?

It was just an idle threat to keep unruly children subdued. You might hear an exasperated Mother on market day say, "You'll be banished!" to her charge. But banishment was not real.

Until now.

William's Mother is about to protest, but the Sentry sweeps past her. William and I are wrenched apart, and the last thing I see is the Sentry herding William and his Mother across the marble Atrium. William is tall and dignified in his crisp white shirt and black pants, and he has his arm around his Mother, helping her out the front door. Then he rolls her down the steep ramp of the Oculum Senate, and out to the common.

He gives me a quick, parting look and mouths two words: THE DOOR.

MANNFRED

The Black Rain finally stopped, but it's the worst rain we ever seen.

It made the river rise, then overflow, then flood us out. It took away the footbridge. We heard a crash, then we looked out the window, and it was floating away in the storm.

Grannie's house is the closest to the footbridge, and on the second night, we heard the river lapping against the porch. We all went up to the attic, after we cleared out the FatRats and their nests. The Littluns slept on the floor, and Grannie and Lisle slept on a straw tick me and Cranker dragged up the ladder.

We didn't get much sleep that night.

When we woke up the next day, the black river water was all over the main floor and raging out the back door and windows. Grannie saved all the food by hanging it from nets in the ceiling the night before, so we won't starve. The henhouse and goat pen were both on higher ground, so the animals were safe, the greenhouse too.

But we couldn't stay in Grannie's house.

The main floor was half under water, and the river

didn't look like it was going to flow away anytime soon. It took a new course and flowed through the house. Grannie called me and Cranker to the neighbors, and we all talked about what to do, while the Littluns ran wild in the neighbor's nice house. (Much nicer than Grannie's, since they didn't have Littluns.) The neighbors said they'd take care of the greenhouse, and Grannie's house and goats and chickens, but there was nowhere for us to stay. The rest of the houses in our village belonged to people who came back now and then. Some of the houses were good and empty but belonged to people who got Dying Fever and went for good, so their houses were too busted down now to live in for long.

There was no choice; we got to leave.

So Grannie said we were going to the City to stay with her brother. He's got land and houses and animals, room enough for us all. And no Littluns of his own.

Cranker was excited about going, leaving our home behind us, maybe forever. I couldn't tell him I wasn't, or he'd tease me. The Littluns all seemed excited too, but what did they know about anything? All I could think was: what's the City? I knew it was big, with more people than I ever seen in my life, and far away. But what was it like? Were people kind and good? Or would we have to fight and who knows what to get along?

I couldn't ask Grannie, though, she was too busy. So I kept quiet and scowled for the next two days while we got ready to leave the only home I ever known behind us.

We packed up the grain, the oats, the precious dried meat, into the metal locker the Shiny Man left us. We rolled up our beds and blankets in big bundles. Grannie put all her cloth, scissors, knives, kitchen pots and pans, and other shiny into a wooden crate covered by heavy, waterproof oilcloth.

She started a huge fire in the fireplace of the biggest empty house in the village that still had most of a roof and heated water from the village pump for the tin bath. Then Cranker and me caught each Littlun and scrubbed him until we could see skin and not dirt. Then we scrubbed and washed ourselves.

It was an exhausting day, packing up and cleaning everyone. I never been so tired, plus my head felt weird after I used Grannie's black soap to wash out the lice and muck of the past year. I felt like I lost my skin, and Cranker and me laughed at each other, how different we looked with clean faces and hair. After we were clean, Grannie lined us up and cut all our hair off with her new scissors, and that felt even worse. My head was too light, my neck too bare, I could see too much, hear too well.

The Littluns were all quiet, like they could never remember being clean before. They looked at themselves in the big cracked mirror in the abandoned upstairs of the house we were using, laughing and giggling and pushing each other. Grannie threatened them all with no dinner if anyone rolled in the mud.

Then she gave us all a surprise. After we were clean

and standing in new long johns and undershirts she gave us, she unrolled a bundle, and there were new trousers for me and Cranker and new shirts she sewed from the soft blue flannel the Shiny Man gave her. They fit us both a little large, since they had room for a year of growing, but I wasn't complaining.

She was always knitting or sewing, all the nights I had ever known her, and she surprised us all some more with new brown and blue woolen sweaters, one each. She had new overalls for the Littluns, which she scrubbed and patched from second-hand ones the Shiny Man left her. She even had new overalls for herself and new black boots. My feet were always sore from boots too small for me, and she surprised me with a new pair of leather boots as well.

They were a little big, but I never had new leather boots before, and I stared down at my feet like a Littlun. I was worried I was going to start to cry, but Cranker got mad because he had to wear my old boots, which fit him, and so I forgot about it. Our soiled old clothes, the ones Grannie couldn't clean or save, went into a sack to be tore into rags. There was never anything wasted.

When we were all lined up in front of her, with clean faces, short hair, and new clothes, Grannie smiled at us.

"You look like a boys' choir from Cambridge," she said. She lost a tooth at the front last year, so her smile looked a little dark, but it was still good. It's a rare thing to see Grannie smile. I got no idea what a boys' choir or Cambridge might be, but I was glad we could make Grannie smile.

We slept in the abandoned house with the leaky roof that night, then the next day Cranker and me helped Grannie get the cart loaded with all our worldly goods. Grannie picked the best nanny goat out of her small herd and two good egg-laying hens from the henhouse. The rest she left for the neighbors to take care of, and to use as they saw fit. They promised to use them well and to keep them going for us if we ever returned, and to share the goods with the Shiny Man and other travelers who ever came by the village. They would keep the beans, carrots, and vetch going in the greenhouse. Then we hugged the neighbors goodbye, laced our two old nags, Nancy and Nellie, into the harness, and lifted the Littluns, the goat, and the hens into the cart. The baby Lisle sat up front with Grannie, strapped to her with the blue sling.

Cranker and me sat at the back of the cart, keeping our feet out of the water as we forded the river and left our little village behind. Grannie's house got smaller and smaller as we got onto higher ground and a drier track. The neighbor waved goodbye out her second floor window, and I watched until we went over a rise and I didn't see her or our little village anymore.

I been away from there twice in my life: the time before I arrived at Grannie's, which I don't remember because I was such a Littlun.

And now.

I turn my head because I can't let Cranker see my tears.

Grannie drives the cart, and it rocks and rolls along as Nancy and Nellie pull us on the log-and-mud track over the dark fields. Pretty soon, all the Littluns fall asleep, even Lisle in the blue sling under Grannie's arm, with the wooden soother I made in her mouth.

There's once in a while an abandoned farmhouse to look at, their windows all broke and their roofs caved in. Doors and fences and anything useful have all been stripped and used elsewhere. There's sometimes a small village like our own, old houses and a fence with goats and henhouses, but we don't see many people. Just a farmer now and then, working in a field with horses or maybe by hand. They look up at us, sometimes wave, sometimes not.

We have to be wary and watch careful.

Grannie put me and Cranker at the back for a reason. Cranker's got his slingshot and a pocket of rocks ready. I got my knife, which I can throw if I have to, since I practiced enough with it now. And at the front of the slow cart, with all our goods, Littluns and a baby girl, Grannie has the Shiny Man's gun with five bullets deep in her overalls pocket. She showed us before we pulled away from her house but put her finger to her lips in a *shhh, be quiet, don't tell* way. The Littluns would only be curious and pester her for it.

We aren't traveling a dangerous road. There are a few

other people around too, but you never know what you might come across, as Grannie says.

We sit like that all day, covering league after league. Cranker falls asleep, and I know that other than Grannie, I'm the only one awake. I'm glad he's asleep, though, because we got a shadow.

The scrawny, one-eyed dog trots along the ditches and black grass of the mud track, following us all the way. Sometimes he criss-crosses the road, sometimes I don't see him for a while, but he's there all right. Once I see him dart past the back of the cart with a FatRat in his mouth, and once, when the cart stops and we lift all the Littluns down to make water in the ditch and to walk the goat and eat a little bread, I see him lying in the grass, his one good eye on me. As soon as he spies me, he wags the end of his tail. He's getting better at letting just me see him and hiding from the others. That's why he's still alive, most like. Maybe he's not so stupid.

We travel in the cart for two days and nights, only stopping to rest and water the horses or to stretch our legs and eat. No one bothers us, though people do travel along this muddy track to get to and from the City. The Shiny Man would have come along here with his horse and wagon, stopping at farms and villages along the way. We don't see him, or anyone like us, though, just the lone farmers and their goats and hens.

On the third day, at dusk, Grannie drives the cart onto a bridge over a big river. The horse's hooves strike brick, which is loud and different from the drumming on the dirt track.

We all wake up and stare. There are torches lit and wagons overturned. There are people, probably thirty at least, more than I ever seen all at once, standing around. They're all ages, men and women, some older than Grannie. There's a group of boys and girls too, about the same age as me and Cranker, or maybe a little older, throwing rocks at a tree.

Grannie pulls the horses up and we stop in the torch-light. The crowd of strangers at the gate turn to us in the twilight, and my skin starts to itch. All those eyes seem like questions, and we got a lot of answering to do.

Above us, two pillars stand taller than trees. A huge shiny gate big as a house rests open, and a line of carts, horses, and people wait there. Towering buildings crowd all around us, but the windows are all gone, the doors too. The first stars shine through the split and fallen roofs.

We heard of buildings, of course, but seeing them, that's a different thing. I had no way to imagine how big or busted and strange they are. The sun sets over a world of falling buildings and rubble, and I can't make sense of it.

We're at the mighty gates of the City. And I never seen anything so huge or terrifying. Nor ever dreamed of it, but I will now, until the end of my days.

MIRANDA1

The Black Rain has stopped, but I still feel a darkness around me.

William1 and I do not speak again. I see him in Teaching Hall and at the Seed Park from far away, but he doesn't approach me or seek me out. I miss him. But we must keep apart. I do not want to be banished, whatever that means. I don't want him to be banished, either.

Then a few days after Regulus gave us his dire warning, we are both in Teaching Hall, helping the youngest children learn their letters. Either Regulus has decided not to separate us or he is testing us. We deliberately sit at opposite ends of the room and do not look at one another. The children are Annas and Andrews, the four-year-olds and the youngest of Oculum. They were the last children to be awoken, which is interesting. The nursery is now empty and all the Nursies taken apart, since they can be recycled into Mothers; they share many of the same parts.

But William and I have often spoken of this. What will happen now there are no more infants to awaken? No more of the youngest to raise? All of us, all one thousand children of Oculum, are now awake. It feels final, like the end of something. But the end of what?

The Teacher has finished reading from the WillBook. Today he has been reading the story of a girl with the same name as me, Miranda, and the enchanted island she lives upon. It is one of my favorite stories, but we never hear the ending, so I don't know how it works out. The Teacher returns the WillBook to safekeeping beneath the thick glass cover. He has left it open, and one by one the children go up and look at it through the glass. They pick out letters if they can, a word if they are beginning to read. Jake47 must have been very determined to get his hand under there and touch it.

I sit with Andrew34. He's having a hard time with the letter "J." He keeps drawing it backward, like a hook, and I patiently take his small hand and trace the correct shape with it and get him to do it again. Backward. I've seen four-year-olds do this before, of course, but he may need extra assistance. The Teacher is quite good and patient with children who have problems with letters and numbers. I may have to summon the Teacher's help for Andrew34 in the coming weeks.

I take a quick look at William1. He is showing his table of children a magic trick. He holds out a pebble then closes his palm over it, waves his other hand over it, and opens his palm again.

The pebble is gone.

It's a simple trick, and I smile at the children's wonder.

William1 catches my eye, smiles, then goes back to the children and settles them to practice reading. The Sentry doesn't notice our quick look.

Someone touches my arm, and I turn to face a tiny child with a yellow armband and a silver "A12." Anna12. She hands me a folded piece of heavy paper with my name on the outside, written in a childish hand.

"Miranda1, I have made this for you."

"Thank you, Anna12," I answer. She curtseys and hides a shy smile then scampers back to the other side of the room and sits beside William1. He seems not to have noticed. Children often give me drawings and stories in Teaching Hall, so it's not unusual. I peek inside the folded paper and then quietly put the drawing into my satchel.

There's a letter inside the drawing. The letter is folded and plain, but I have no doubt what it is.

A note from William1.

I peek at the Sentry beside the door, which hasn't paid much attention to me. It looks at me, but only because I am looking at it. This is something new, having a Sentry follow me. I have never been followed before, and it's becoming tiresome. Regulus didn't mention that he was going to have us followed.

When Teaching Hall is over, I leave the room at the end of the line of fifty Annas. William lines up to leave the Hall at the back of the fifty Andrews. I walk past the Sentry with my head up. William is bent down to help Andrew21 tie his shoe. When he stands, he takes the child's hand and walks out the door without a look in my direction.

I get home, but Mother is not there. She must be at the market or perhaps tending to her squeaky wheels. I finally made an appointment for her with Toolman, which was earlier today. I go up to my bedroom and sit with my back against the door (for some reason this seems very important, to block the door), and with shaking hands I open Anna12's drawing.

It is a tree garden, a child's rendition of the Seed Park. And there, at the very edge of the picture, behind clumsy, curling roses, is a tiny, perfectly drawn door. William must have added the door to the child's picture. You almost wouldn't see it unless you knew to look for a door in that spot.

I start to breathe quickly and take out the folded letter.

The child's shaky handwriting traces William's large, elegant letters. The letter simply says, "*Dear Miranda1, I dream I will visit the Seed Park with you. Anna12.*" I look back at the picture again and peer closely at the roses almost touching the door.

There! A tiny word is hidden among the roses in William's writing!

It says, "Tonight."

I light a candle, since it is getting dark out. Even though the Black Rain has stopped, Regulus still has not opened Oculum, so there is no moon, no stars shining down. I take the lit candle and the child's drawing and letter with me into the water closet and lock the door. Then I burn all evidence of the letter and the picture. The ash falls into the wash basin, and I mix it slowly with water from the jug, then I watch as it gurgles down the drain.

I have never been sneaky. I have never given a thought to secret letters or meetings or doorways into the unknown. Up until a few days ago, my life was perfect. Quiet. Even dull. But something tells me, a little voice perhaps that I didn't know I had, whispers that no one must read the letter or see the child's drawing. There is something else that also whispers to me: you must go out tonight, sneak past Mother and the Sentry, and meet William1 *at the door.*

I have no idea how I am going to achieve this.

No one goes out after dark, unless it is a scheduled event. Sometimes, when the full moon passes over Oculum and it is good weather, Regulus will open our world and the children and their Mothers will all gather on the common to watch. Or sometimes, after a long season of games, all the children will assemble on the common to watch the final games and celebrate the winners. This is a festival and always takes place under the floodlit firmament after dark. Again, when a section of the Seed Park comes into fruit, and the Treekeepers have picked all the trees clean, we gather as a community after dark and light candles and walk to the Seed Park together. We sing songs, we rejoice, and it's a celebration.

But we never, ever, wander on the streets after dark unaccompanied unless we have a terrible emergency, such as illness or fire, or a Mother has broken down for good. If we are scheduled to visit with each other or go on an errand after dark, our Mother would always accompany us.

I sit through my dinner, soup and dried cherries for dessert, without eating a bite. Mother rumbles around the kitchen and hums quietly, a habit of hers I've never really liked. No one else's Mother hums, not as far as I can tell. Since the meeting with Regulus, she hasn't said much to me. I can tell she is worried, and I think her silence may be because she doesn't want to intrude or bother me.

If I am in love, as she, William's Mother, and Regulus believe, she may be hoping that I shall discuss it. She has always been very good at leaving me alone until I bring whatever is bothering me up on my own.

I appreciate her tact, but she'll be waiting a long time to hear from me about this.

How would I discuss an utterly forbidden meeting at a *secret door* with someone I am supposed to *love*?

I don't eat much, I do some reading, I say good-night as early as I can without seeming ill and causing alarm, and then I go to my bedroom. Shortly afterward, Mother comes and tucks me in.

"Goodnight, Mother," I say.

"Goodnight, Miranda my darling," she says. She gives

me her usual cool, metallic hug. She whirrs around the bed and does some final blanket tucking, then she hesitates at the door. She turns and whispers in her cranky, mechanical voice, "I do not know what love is exactly, Miranda my darling, but I do *not* think it can be so very evil."

I'm shocked at this. Mother rarely shares thoughts with me; in fact, I have often wondered if she has thoughts of her own. A Mother is not a creature who is required to deliver much thought on anything, except how to keep her charge clean, fed, and safe. William believes they have no other purpose than to feed and clothe us, their children. But sometimes my Mother surprises me.

"Thank you, Mother dear," I say. She gives her wobbly smile, then she closes my door, and I hear the door to her closet shut. I know she will close herself down for the night and only awaken before 7:00 a.m. if I call her.

As soon as I am sure she has shut down completely, I reach under my bed and pull out the clothes I have assembled there: my long, black frock, my black leggings, black shoes, and long black hooded cloak. I dress as quietly as I can in the dark. Then I pull the cork seal from a water jug and hold it over the lit candle. I draw the charred cork across my hands, across my face. I hope I am invisible to the Sentries and to anyone else, but I have never done this before, so I have no idea if I am or not.

I slip downstairs, pull up my hood, and slide out into the night.

MANNFRED

We been waiting so long to get through the City gate that the sun sets. The moon shines down and stars glow through busted windows in the buildings all around us. I can't see the buildings in the darkness now too well, but the view I got at sundown was enough to set me trembling.

There's a wide track made of bricks, or something close to bricks, Grannie calls a road. We sit under the wagon. Nancy and Nellie are loose in their harness, standing and sleepy. The Littluns are stuck close to me and Cranker, dozing. Grannie waits to talk to the people at the gate, but she has to be patient. Other carts, other people, wait too, like us.

There are men and women with clubs and knives that guard the gate. They carry torches and seem in charge. The tallest man among them, a big, powerful man in every way, does all the talking, or most of it. Seems everyone who goes into the City got to talk to him first.

But it's a slow business, and Grannie waits her turn.

Grannie didn't say anything about these giant gates or about what the City looks like in the dark with all those towering, busted-up buildings. Or about these guards.

Maybe she didn't tell us because we'd be scared. But I'm scared anyway, telling or not.

There are other carts and wagons. One cart has just one man, and he goes through the gates quick. Seems that carts with families like us must wait. Everyone carries sacks, cloth, food, animals, some even have shiny with them. My head spins from all the watching.

Cranker and me been watching a gang of thieves, too. They're four of them, older girls and boys, Cranker's age or older maybe, but none as big as me. They steal from a cart when no one is looking, a sack of carrots here, a hammer there. They reach in and grab as the cart goes by then run to stow whatever they took behind a big tree.

No one seems to notice but me and Cranker.

At last the tall man and his crew come to our cart with torches in hand and tell us all to stand up. It's our turn. Grannie puts Lisle into my arms, and I throw the blue sling over my shoulder and hold her like Grannie does, under my arm and against my chest.

The Littluns all stand silent and close around me and Cranker, half asleep in the torchlight. I pull a few thumbs out of sleepy mouths. First time I ever seen them all silent at the same time. They all take a hand or grab a piece of my shirt, and they even hold Cranker's hands, and he lets them. We're all quiet and terrified.

The tall man talks to Grannie. I never seen her look so serious. Far as I can hear, her answers are "Yes sir," and "No sir," mostly. The rest of the tall man's crew comes and look through our belongings. They shine torches on Nancy and Nellie, who shy away, and then they take all our bundles out of the cart and paw through them. They find Grannie's shiny and take the new pair of scissors, some of the blue flannel cloth she used for our shirts. They take the goat and one of the hens. Then they come over and look close at me, Cranker, and the Littluns.

A guard shines a torch in my face and peers at Lisle in the sling.

"Whose baby is that?" she demands. She's fearsome, tough as nails and stringy as one of Grannie's old hens, even though she's so tiny and I'm so tall, she has to tilt her head right back to see me. The group of thieves stand at the edge of the torchlight, and I catch a grin off one of them. The leader. His head is shaved, and now he's closer I see he's missing front teeth. The thieves remind me of skinny wolves, waiting for something to happen.

"She's my little sister," I say, shaking. Grannie has told me to say this: if anyone stops us on the road, we're to say that Cranker and me are brothers and Lisle our sister. The Littluns are our brothers and cousins, though we're all so different, all colors and sizes, I can't see anyone believing it.

"What's her name?"

"Lisle."

"How old is she?" The guard looks at me then sticks her finger in Lisle's mouth. Lisle opens her eyes to whine, but I stuff the soother back in her mouth, and she settles.

"She was born harvest last, so she's just over five months, that's why she's got no teeth yet," I say. Grannie has told me to say this, too.

"And who's the woman you're with? Your ma?"

"No ma'am, she's my grandma," I say. The guard holds the torch close to my face, looks me in the eye, then does the same with Cranker and each Littlun in turn, like she's looking for something. Then she goes back to the tall man talking to Grannie, and says, "They's no relation. Not one of them looks like the other."

Grannie keeps talking to the man, serious and low, and the guard walks away with the torch. I take a breath, then turn to say something to Cranker, and ... where's Cranker? I dart to the corner of the cart, and Lisle complains. The Littluns follow me in a cloud.

There's Cranker, his slingshot hard against the shaved head of the thief leader with the missing teeth. The thief is still, but he's got Grannie's last hen under his arm.

"Put it back," Cranker hisses, and the boy moves slow and puts the hen back in the cart.

"Get," Cranker hisses again, and his menace even scares me. The thief smirks, then bumps into me and looks up. I'm taller; it'll always be that way.

I'll always be taller than most.

The thief gobs up at me, and hot spit hits my face. Then he laughs and runs off to his thieving gang, who rumble a few curses at us on their way. I'm too surprised to do anything but make sure Lisle is okay then wipe away spit.

"He's gonna plague us next time," Cranker mutters.

"What makes you think there'll be a next time?" I ask, walking the stunned Littluns back to the other side of the cart.

"There'll be a next time, Mann," he says. Cranker has wisdom sometimes, and I know he's right. Just one more thing in the City to fear.

I look over, and Grannie says something else too low to hear to the tall man. Then I see the precious gun slide from her hand to his. He hides the gun and the handful of bullets in his coat then turns to us.

"Gather your belongings and go."

We get everything back into the cart quick and count the Littluns to make sure we don't leave one behind (I'm scared enough to), then Cranker and me get into the back and Grannie starts Nellie and Nancy up, and we pass through the huge gates.

The last thing I see is Grannie's prize nanny goat being led away and her precious hen already turning on a spit over a fire. The toothless thief rubs his hands over the fire with his gang. He looks up and catches my eye and spits again. I'm too far to feel it, but I do feel the memory of it, hot on my face, all the same.

I only stop shaking when we leave those gates behind us. We drive on another hour into the dark City.

When we stop in a quiet place between some small

buildings, houses maybe, but it's hard to see in the dark, I ask Grannie why the guards took the scissors, the goat, and the hen. I don't mention the gun. It scares me that she gave it away to open the gates to us. Our passing through the gates took a long time, longer than most, and I saw the tall man and the guard look over at me and Lisle, again and again. Babies are rare, girl babies most of all, but not rare as guns.

Grannie says, grim, "Just be thankful that's all they took, Mann. The cost of safe passage and not so high. What's a goat, a hen, a pair of scissors, compared to the life of a child?"

I wonder at this. It's true, there aren't that many Littluns in the world, and even then not all of them end up in families that can feed them. The lucky ones, like me, Cranker, Lisle, our other Littluns, find their way to someone like Grannie. The unlucky ones? I guess they find themselves traded at the gates and left behind.

Cranker and me rub down the horses, feed them a bag of oats each, and find water from a hand pump we see others use. Grannie feeds us, we get carrots, fresh water and hard-baked bread that takes a lot of spit to soften. Then she puts the Littluns to bed in the cart, and Cranker and me fall asleep exhausted under it, listening to Grannie singing soft to all of us.

We're in a quiet space away from the road, something Grannie calls a "courtyard." There's another family in a cart with mules near us. I have no idea if this is a safe place. Grannie says it is but to keep my knife close and Cranker's slingshot, too.

The one-eyed dog slips past the cart just as I fall asleep and rests in a doorway, watching over us all night. Somehow I'm glad he's here, something from home no one took yet.

What did he pay the guards to get through? More than likely he's got nothing they want. He's one of the lucky ones.

MIRANDA 1

The streets are silent.

It's dark, since Regulus has turned off the lights in the firmament, and Oculum is closed tight. I can see the Senate in the distance and the dim outline of houses and trees. This is the way the night has always seemed from safely inside my bedroom. But it is a different thing to be wandering the dark streets of Oculum alone for the first time in my life.

There are noises, small shufflings, scurryings, and gentle sighs that I have never noticed before. Suddenly I feel like a small child, like Jake47, frightened of Fandoms, and I cannot stop the memories and whisperings about those strange images passing beyond our world, half-seen monsters wriggling and wavering against the wall of Oculum.

But we are told by our Mothers, by Regulus, that there are no such things as Fandoms. That there is no Outside, only the stars and the moon above.

But now there is William's door.

If the door is opened ... what awaits?

I almost wish he hadn't shown it to me. I draw the

hood closely over my face and walk as silently as I can across the street, along the sidewalk, between two houses (Gisele37's and Simon50's) until I come to the common. I skirt the trees, past the great marble stairs and the square in front of the Oculum Senate. I have made up a story: if I'm stopped, I'll say that I am unwell and on my way to visit the Medicus alone, since I was unable to wake Mother. If she is questioned, she would be alarmed, but I'm sure she would play along. I can act delirious or short of breath, or perhaps I will faint. I'm sure the worst that a Sentry would do is march me home or make me talk to Regulus.

There doesn't seem to be a Sentry following me, which gives me pause. Even though I stood perfectly still in the bushes outside my house for several minutes, no Sentry appeared. So I can only assume that the Sentry does not expect me to slip out of my house unaccompanied at night because such a thing is unheard of.

William1 and I are taking a terrible risk. I do not wish to be banished.

Banished. What is it? And *where* is it? Perhaps it means that if we are caught, we will be alone, separated, banished from the company of everyone else. Even though I do not truly know what Regulus means by it, it strikes terror in me.

I stick to the tree-lined outskirts of the common and cross to the cherry-tree-lined walkway along the main street of Oculum. The cherry trees will soon be in full blossom. I slip quietly past the Punishment Hall, the Teaching Hall, the Food Hall, past the shops for Market Day. I pass the Medicus Hall where we go for regular checkups of our height and weight, or if we are hurt or ill. Our Medicus team is clever and can mend bones and tend our ailments very well. They teach us how to tend others, as well.

I've heard of a thing called death. Teacher has taught us about it, but I've never seen it.

No one has ever died in Oculum.

Then I pass the Tailor's shop and the Cobbler's shop, and I slip past the Toolman's warehouse. The grounds around the warehouse are filled with broken-down Mothers and partially dismantled Nursies, which we don't need any more now that the Andrews and Annas have left the nursery. There are some broken Sentries as well, and the effect of the mechanical arms, wheels, and grinning faces in the half-dark is odd and ghoulish. It looks perfectly ordinary by day, but I have never considered it at night, alone.

I quicken my pace.

So far I've seen no one.

I catch the scent of blossoms. I'm near the Seed Park. The lights in the firmament above are low, since the fruit trees need to rest, but it is not completely dark over the park. As I draw near, I can see the outline of trees; the bushes and flowers stand out in the low light.

There are no Treekeepers working in the fruit trees. I can't see William1 anywhere.

I am alone.

This is the most dangerous part of my journey. The lights are low, but they're on. I'll be seen plainly by anyone who is near. I wait behind a small oak tree, a sapling, and scan the park for a moment, but there is no movement. I can see the rose-covered trellis, and I slowly, slowly make my way there, taking cover behind fruit trees, behind bushes, behind a greenhouse, behind a light pole. At one point I do see a Sentry, but it's a good way off and turns and wheels the other way.

The last few steps to the rose bush trellis are made in full light, but there's nothing I can do about this. I wait until the Sentry is out of sight, then I dash to the rose bush.

William is not here.

My heart pounds. What if he's been caught? What if I misunderstood his message on Anna12's drawing, and he isn't coming? I can see the curved wall of Oculum in the distance. It's not that far. A short run and I could leap the perimeter fence and dash to the door.

And then what?

Suddenly I realize how foolish this is. What can I hope to achieve? What was I thinking?

"Miranda." A whisper.

"Miranda, over here." William1 is so well camouflaged in black shirt, pants, black shoes, and cloak that I can barely see him. He is standing almost at the perimeter fence, next to the tall black walnut tree. I can see the crown and the branches of this tree from my house, it is so vast. Some branches almost touch the wall. This is the tree that all twelve-year olds must climb, using a special lightweight ladder for the occasion, in the annual coming-of-age festival. It's a long way up, a view I will always remember from my twelfth year, since I almost fell.

He waves at me to join him, but I'm frozen to the spot. A Sentry slowly wheels toward us. I can't tell if it has seen William or not, but it certainly will if it continues along its path.

William hasn't seen the Sentry and waves at me again. I shake my head and nod toward the Sentry. I don't think the guard can see me, but I'm not sure. William sees the Sentry, too, and lengthens against the dark trunk of the tree. At the last moment, the Sentry turns and wheels back the way it came, slowly traveling the curve of the wall away from us.

William waves at me again, and I dash to the walnut tree.

"William, this is so dangerous. What are we doing here?" I'm afraid my whisper is a shout. I can hardly keep my voice down.

"Shhh." He draws his arm across my shoulder, a gesture of affection.

"It's dangerous, but we have to find out more about

the door. It's inconceivable that there is a door in the wall. No Teacher, Nursie, or Mother has ever mentioned it, Regulus never has either, and yet ... there it is." William looks at me. His is a sweet face, a trustworthy face, a face I've known all my life. He's got a few reddish hairs showing along his jawline, the first time I've noticed them. His dark eyes shine in the half-light.

"I'm sorry, Miranda. I know I've dragged you into this. I told Regulus we were hiding together, we were in love, because that was the *only* thing I could say that he might not question. I didn't want him to realize that we'd found the door." I nod.

"But why haven't we seen it before?" I ask. This has been troubling me. It doesn't make sense.

"We haven't seen it before because we were too short to see over the rose bush. I've grown lately, and so have you. When the Treekeepers pruned this area a few weeks ago, I caught sight of the top of the door and then got closer and closer each day until I could see all of it."

"Well, why is there a door, anyway?" I ask.

William looks at me tenderly. "Someone put the door there, a long time ago. Someone wants us to walk through it."

"No, William!" I cannot believe he has just said this. I look down at my hands in shock. He looks around, no Sentry in sight, and goes on quietly.

"Regulus threatened us with banishment, Miranda. Haven't you wondered about that? Banishment? Where would they banish us to? Where else is there but Oculum?"

"Banishment? I thought it might mean separating us, making us live alone."

William shakes his head and looks toward the door. "Miranda, it is something much more."

He reaches into his cloak and pulls out a slim book with gold lettering on the front cover: *For the Children of Oculum.* He opens it and shows me the first page and there, written in a beautiful hand, are the words that we all learn from Teacher: *"We have given you every plant seed, and every tree which has fruit; it will be food for you."*

He slips the book back into his cloak and whispers, "Mother gave this book to me two days ago. She has always had it and has been waiting to give it to me on the day that I first speak of love."

"How did she know that day would come?"

William gets a wild look in his eye. "There are so many answers in this book, Miranda. As the oldest child of Oculum, it was given to my Mother to give to me when the time was right. Have you not always wondered about love? About death? About why the Mothers, the Sentries, Regulus, why they are so different from us? About the sky above, the stars that shine? It's all here." William is breathless, overexcited, and I try to calm him. I put my hand on his shoulder.

"SHHH! But what's in it?" My heart pounds harder. William is starting to raise his voice. We are head-to-head, and he forces his voice back to a whisper.

"Miranda, there is a world outside. *Outside* is real. One of us has to go through the door to see it. One of us has to watch." As soon as he says it … it's obvious. A door is meant to be opened. I swallow my fear.

"William, it's just a book. You cannot go out that door. You have no idea what's out there. If there *is* anything out there."

William shakes his head again. "When Oculum is open, Miranda, what do you see?"

"Stars, clouds, sky, the moon, the sun. What else would I see?"

William looks wildly over my head. The Sentry has turned and is wheeling our way!

"There's no time! The book has told me so much, Miranda. I have written some of the truth of it on the back of the Map of Oculum in my house. If anything happens to me, you must get the map and read it. Promise me!"

"William, what are you talking about? Your map?" I know the map. He's worked on it since he was small, a huge, intricate, carefully exact map of all the houses, buildings, and trees in Oculum. It's been his life's work.

"And what do you mean *if anything happens to me*?" My heart thuds painfully in my ears. He takes my face in his hands. The Sentry is closer.

"I am going to the door. I am going to push upon it. If it opens, I shall walk through."

"But you'll be caught. And *banished*," I whisper. The last word catches in my throat. I want to talk him out of it. I want to leave and go home, right now. There is still a chance we may get out of this without getting caught.

Then our future is decided for us.

The Sentry sees William.

"Goodbye, Miranda!"

William kisses me on the cheek, then he dashes across the open park toward the wall. The Sentry blows its whistle and churns to top speed. I've never seen a Sentry move at top speed.

It's fast. Faster than I could have imagined.

But William is fast too, and in a moment he vaults over the perimeter fence. The Sentry speeds forward, wheels a blur, whistle howling, and William sprints to the door.

He pushes upon it … nothing happens.

The Sentry is almost upon him. Another Sentry has wheeled into view in the distance, and another. They blow their whistles, too, and lurch forward as they pick up speed. William pushes upon the door again, frantic, and this time it moves. It opens wide, and just as the Sentry reaches for him … William steps through the door.

The door slowly closes behind him and shuts with a click.

I leap out of my hiding place.

"NO!" I'm fully exposed in the light, and the Sentries turn and stare at me. William is forgotten. It's almost as though he was never there, since none of the Sentries moves to reopen the door.

Instead they only focus upon me.

I let the Sentries come. I don't even try to run away. What would be the point? I stare at the door as it closes. In the next second, I see William's face through the curved, opaque wall of my world. William leans into the wall and looks at me from wherever he is.

From Outside. Outside the door.

His eyes are huge. His teeth leap out of his head, distorted. He puts an enormous hand against the wall, and his hand leaps and jumps like a monstrous, terrifying shadow up the wall.

The Sentries are upon me and grab an arm, a shoulder, another arm. We turn and march and wheel across the grass of the Seed Park. All this happens as if in a dream, though. The only clear thought I have runs through my head again and again: William opened the door and walked through it. William is Outside.

Outside is real.

Fandoms are real people.

And William is a Fandom.

MANNFRED

I wake up to a whine.

The one-eyed dog sits just out of reach. I see his paws and chest from where I lie under the cart. When I stir, he whines again and dips his head low so we can look at each other. Then he whines with a tiny growl mixed in, too, and disappears like a shadow. His black paws run away out of sight.

It's early light, and no one else is awake. I want to wake Cranker, but he's snoring like he won't wake up. If I wake him when he's snoring like this, I might get a slingshot stone in the face. It's happened.

So I roll out from under the cart … and freeze. Two men stand at the entrance to the courtyard, their backs to me. They creep toward the other cart, toward the family with the mules. The men are big, strong.

The dog is nowhere.

I duck down low and whisper loud as I dare, "Cranker!" I wish I woke him now, but he's not going to wake up. I gulp and look over at the men, who move toward the mules. Mules are rare and sturdy, and it's clear the men plan to steal them.

Our horses, Nancy and Nellie, are standing and sleepy, tied to the cart rail. I move between them so I can see the men. Grannie snores, the Littluns breathe all around her in the cart. Our last hen hears me and rustles in her cage, opens one eye, and goes back to sleep. There's one of Grannie's new metal pots just inside the cart, and I lift it out quiet as anything. I reach in and get down a big soup ladle, too.

The men slip between the mules, and the family on the other side of the courtyard sleeps on. The mules are nervous, but the men soothe them with their hands. They untie the animals. They'll be gone soon.

I stand clear of the horses — I don't need a kicking — and bang on the pot hard as I can with the soup ladle.

CLANG-CLANG-CLANG!

The men whirl around, and I duck down behind Nellie. Grannie wakes, the Littluns set up a howl and a scream, Cranker wakes up with a swear, then bangs his head on the bottom of the cart with another swear.

The men drop the mules and run off, and I go soothe the animals and tie them up again.

The other family wakes up too, and a face pops over the side of their cart and smiles at me. It's a girl. She snaps up her overalls and joins me to say hello. Her pa and ma wake up and thank me, and Grannie comes over and we all shake hands.

The truth is I never seen a girl my own age before. All we ever had in our tiny village of ten houses is boys, and plenty of them. The pa thanks me for saving the mules, and I'm all of a sudden blushing and shy. I must have shown it, because when we leave the place an hour later, Cranker won't stop teasing me about the girl.

"Manny Mann got a girlfriend!" he says, all gleeful and making smooch noises. I take a few swipes at him, but he dances away and goes on teasing until he gets bored and drops it.

We walk beside the cart now, following the old road through the edge of the City toward the center. It's a long way to where Grannie's brother lives. We got to walk three or four days clear to the other side to get there. Grannie drives the cart slow, and Cranker and me keep the Littluns from wandering off, walking them along like a herd of ornery goats. They got so much energy, we have to run them for a least some of the day or they'll gnaw off their own feet with boredom.

The buildings around us now are houses, and some bigger ones that Grannie calls "apartments." People lived together in them in the Olden Begones, but most of them are falling apart slow, tumbling into themselves, or slanting over and crumbling into the street. Some lean on the buildings next to them. Grannie tells us that glass and brick get swept out of the way when a building falls to keep the road open to carts and foot traffic, but most of the buildings aren't safe to live in now or for as long as anyone can remember.

There are a few people on the road, families in carts

like ours, with mules, or horses, or even great, slow, lumbering oxen. Or most often just a man on a horse, or a woman with a small, fast cart. Some carts go the same way as us, into the City, and some go the other way, back out to wherever they're from. Trade goes on here in places called "markets," Grannie says, where people trade farm animals and grain and get what the Shiny Man brings us, like knives, and pots and such. My head spins from side to side, there's so much to see. I likely seen fifty new people today, more than my whole life.

There are old piles of junk all along the road, too, big pieces and small. Some of it I understand, most of it I don't. There are busted wagons like the Shiny Man's everywhere, but the rubber wheels are gone, and other machines that we can't imagine what they might be. Huge machines with diggers at the front, or at the back, or with strange round rollers on them, or other things that make no sense, like wagons but giant, with seats for many people. Some of them been busted up and used for shiny, others are just faded and warped, on the side of the road. As we walk along, and the sun rises and the day starts, the wagons and the huge machines rot beside the roads below the tumble-down houses, as far as I can see.

And there's more leftovers from the Olden Begones.

Along the roadside there are careful stacks of strange boxes, what Grannie says is garbage, but not like any I ever seen in our midden back home. This is special garbage, collected here for people to scour. It's boxes in all sizes, in huge numbers. Some of the boxes are flat and open in the middle on a smart hinge. Cranker brought me one, and when I opened it, there was a bunch of letters and numbers about the size of the end of my finger on the bottom part. I picked out an "A" and "S" and "D" on the left side in the middle, and a "Q" and "W" and "E" and "R" and "T" on the left and top. There were strange words, too: "Enter," and "Insert," and "Delete," which made sense, and "PgUp," "PrtSc," and "Num Lock," that didn't.

The rest of the letters were busted or missing.

"What's 'qwert?'" I say. I know the letters, but there's no sense to them. We can't figure it out. They aren't boxes for carrying. They aren't useful for anything that we can see, but in some places they're piled up against the buildings like water. They meant something important to the Olden Begones.

Cranker and me pick these flat boxes up and open them, here and there in the careful stacks all along the road, until we get bored since we can see no point to them. Once in a while a person stands in the garbage, stripping out wires or copper from the bigger boxes, so maybe there's some use to them. Some people even sit and wait beside the road to trade a length of wire they stripped for an egg or a few carrots, to save us the trouble. If a body needed wire to tie up old scissors, or copper for pots or some other shiny, they'd find it in these endless garbage stacks.

There are smaller, flat boxes that fit in a hand, too. They're made of shiny, or what must have been glass once upon a time, or something else that's not quite either. Grannie pays no attention when I hold one up to her in the cart. She stares straight ahead and says it's nothing useful. Just more Olden Begones junk.

But I can't help thinking she knows more than she's saying, so I ask her again and she spies me with her dark blue eye and says, "It's an old way of sending messages, Mann. A useless magic from the Olden Begones."

They were interested in this magic, I think, it's everywhere. But it didn't save them from the Black Rain, the fevers, or the end of fruit trees.

I find one of the small boxes, not all busted up, that fits perfect in my hand. I heft it, like a stone. It has a flat, smooth side and a glass eye on the other, and a shape I see on lots of the boxes: a kind of circle with a piece missing. I show the small box to Grannie and ask her what the shape is.

She tries to ignore me but answers after she sees I won't quit. "It's the shape of an apple, Mann, with a bite out of it." I think about this, curious. The Olden Begones people must have thought apples were important, since the shape is everywhere on their garbage. But why didn't they do more to save them? There's no answer to this, just another Olden Begones mystery.

We walk farther than I ever walked. Even the Littluns get tired and whiny, and me and Cranker give shoulder rides to the littlest ones or lift them into the cart to rest. We stop for lunch at the side of the road, then we keep walking. The Littluns rest in the cart, and Cranker and me walk beside it. The sun is pale overhead. There's not much warmth in it, since it's still early in the year, but it's good on our faces.

At the end of the day, before the sun goes down and the warmth leaves the City, Grannie pulls the horses into another courtyard, and she sets about dinner while me and Cranker play with the Littluns. There's more carts parked here, another family, and soon our Littluns and the others that are gathered get to playing. Our Littluns are no better or no worse behaved than the others; in fact, they get along with the newcomers. They set to playing rounders, and there's no shouting or pushing at all. I wonder what has come over them? They do seem a little wondering at the new faces, the other Littluns. Maybe the strangeness is making them polite. For now.

The buildings are bigger here, and Grannie says it's since we're close to the center of the City now. The people in the Olden Begones wanted to live near the center, she says, so the buildings got bigger the closer you got. Some of the buildings aren't for living, too. They're just for doing the work of the Olden Begones, whatever that might have been. Those are the tallest. I'm used to them now, so they're not so terrifying to me.

Cranker and me ask if we can explore, and Grannie says yes, don't go far, be back before dark, don't climb high. We set out and walk and walk through the broken down streets and over piles of rubble and tumble-down houses.

After a while, Cranker finds a wide-open doorway and stairs that go down and down into a space that runs off into the dark. There's a sign in the wall at the bottom of the stairs. It's busted up but not too busted to read: *Subway*. We can't see what this deep, empty space is for, but we look far into the dark. There are shiny bars, at least in some places where they're not tore out, that run along each other into the darkness. It's just more Olden Begones magic as far as I can see, but Cranker thinks it must have been for travel. We seen metal bars like this running along the countryside above ground, where people haven't lifted it. The story goes that in the Olden Begones, huge carts ran upon the metal bars, fast and all across the country.

I guess it could be, but down here in this place, did the horses pull the carts in the dark?

We heave a few rocks into the darkness and listen to the sound that comes back to us. "It's a deep cave," I say to Cranker. It makes me nervous.

"Naw, it's long and narrow, not a cave," he answers. "More like a FatRat tunnel. Let's see where it goes." We're about to set out, when a noise comes out of the darkness, a moaning shriek and a snarl. We look at each other then whip back up the stairs to the last rays of the sun.

"Could be a FatRat," Cranker says, but I just grunt. I don't want Cranker to hear my shaky voice. *Not a FatRat, a dying man, more like,* I think.

We walk past more busted houses until we see another open doorway in a big marble building still standing. The door is long gone, and we wander up the stairs in a stone hall, up and up and up. When we can't go higher, we step out onto the long, flat roof.

I never been so high in my life, and I can see far as an eagle. I see all the buildings near and far, to the horizon. The City goes on, and on and on, to the setting sun. Cranker and me stand there, amazed.

And there's something else we can see. In the center of the City, a few days' walk, there's a huge glass dome that rises out of the rubble like a giant, icy mountain. It soars into the sky and reflects the sunset beating on it. Cranker and me watch, too awed to talk. We just watch, and then we see something I'll remember the rest of my days.

The very top of the glass dome starts to move, slow, around and around in a big circle. Even this far, I can hear a gentle hum. The sun sets behind the huge dome, but we can see the top turn, turn, and ever so slow, it rises into the sky.

We watch for a long time. If the Olden Begones had black boxes and magic, then this glass dome with the rising center must be part of it. It couldn't be anything but magic that made it so beautiful and mysterious.

The sun sets behind the dome with the rising top, and the City falls dark.

"We better get back," Cranker says, and he's right, because Grannie told us not to climb the buildings. I don't need a tongue-lashing from Grannie. It would be the first one in years. We walk back to Grannie and the Littluns, all silent. I think we're both too awed to speak.

I keep seeing a black shadow out of the corner of my eye, and I know the one-eyed dog is stalking me, keeping me in sight. I'm getting used to him, my lurking shadow.

Cranker shoots a few FatRats on the way back, so Grannie's not too mad with us. She spits them and roasts them for meat along with the soup. I sit and eat, quiet as anything.

I can't get the image of that dome shining in the sunset out of my mind. While me and Cranker watched, the very top unscrewed and lifted into the sky like a giant eye.

Why was the top open? Who opened it?

Or was it just more ancient magic from the Olden Begones that wouldn't quit?

Me and Cranker agreed: somehow we'll get a closer look at that dome.

MIRANDA1

The Sentries brought me home, and one is waiting by our front door. Mother let me in with a worried look, but she didn't ask any questions. She tucked me in with her usual, "Goodnight, Miranda my darling," then rolled back to her closet. I almost missed her squeaky wheels, but she left silently now that the Toolman has fixed her.

I spend a long, sleepless night in my bed. I can see the Arm from my window, and I can see that Regulus has set it in motion. It rises into the darkness, and the fresh air flows in. The Arm turns slowly and makes a low, deep churning sound.

It has always calmed me to hear the Arm working to open the world to the sky.

But tonight I am nothing but nerves. My William, my best friend and lifelong confidante, is *Outside*. He is gone! I know now that Fandoms are real and are nothing more than people pushing against the wall of Oculum. Which means that there are people Outside.

Outside is real.

I lie in my bed, watching Oculum open to the night, and tears soak my cheeks.

Why has Regulus lied to us? Why has Mother lied? Why has no one told us that Outside is real, and that Fandoms are real people there? Miserable, I wonder over and over: where is William1 now, and how will I ever find him again? I'm the only person in Oculum with these thoughts, and I have never felt so alone.

At first light, I wake and dress. At exactly seven o'clock, Mother wheels in to find me fully dressed and seated on my bed. She hands me a note and clucks and whirrs. I don't need to read it. I know what it is, but I open it anyway.

A summons. It is from Regulus: *"Miranda1 will appear at Oculum Senate before Regulus at nine o'clock. She will come accompanied by the Mother of Miranda1."*

I show the note to Mother and head downstairs. There is a new, fragrant bowl of last year's apples and dried cherries beside the front door, but I cannot bring myself to eat anything. I stand on the front step and look at the open sky beyond the Arm, which is now fully extended. Oculum is open. Fresh air fills my lungs, and the sky above is golden and bright, the sun high and clear. There are clouds, a gentle breeze.

And all of it is Outside.

Children walk past me toward Teaching Hall or to the Medicus, the common, or the Seed Park, wherever it is that their schedule sends them. It is a market day, so the youngest Annas and Andrews walk with their Mothers laden with baskets for fruit, vegetables, herbs, or to find new shoes and clothes, haircuts, whatever their charges might need. When Oculum is newly opened, we are all freed, happy, excited to breathe the fresh air and see the sky, and the children walk past me with a spring in their step. The opening of Oculum raises everyone's spirits.

All but mine.

There is a Sentry at the foot of my stairs, and the children and Mothers sneak quick looks at me as I stand in my black cloak behind it. Some of the younger children even stop and openly stare until their nervous Mothers hurry them along. I don't care what I look like. I know a truth that none of them know.

William1 is gone.

At 8:45, Mother joins me on the step. She's wearing her best cloak, and her purple armband with "M1" embroidered in silver stands out brightly. She takes my arm and bravely leads me down the ramp and to the street. All the children and Mothers we meet give us a quick nod or avoid us. I can only assume it is because of the Sentry that rolls along behind us.

We walk with our heads up toward the Senate. I know Mother must have heard whisperings from other Mothers; although I'm not sure exactly how they do it, I know they have a secret communication about their charges. She must have heard that I am in some sort of trouble, reinforced by the appearance of the Sentry and the fact that today is not a day I am normally scheduled to see Regulus.

I am glad she is with me, Mother. Mine. The only thing I have.

I wheel her up the ramp to the big Senate doors, which swing wide as we enter, and slide silently closed behind us. Mother and I take the route across the quiet marble floor of the Atrium and enter the Senate. The giant Arm is fully extended, and from here the sight of the open sky far above our heads is awe-inspiring. A patch of sunlight falls across the Atrium from above.

Regulus sits on his chair and summons us forward. A Mother waits at his feet, and as we join her, I see it is Mother of William1.

I must remain calm.

Her metallic arms are in chains. I have never seen a Mother in chains before. She says hello to us quickly and turns away. If it is possible for a Mother to look unwell, she has managed to do so.

Regulus sits on his chair above us and looks down at me. "Miranda1. So nice of you to come."

"You are welcome, Regulus. Thank you for inviting me." I try not to look away from his mesmerizing stare.

"You have a busy day ahead of you," he says. My normal schedule today would have William1 and I working in the school with the Simons and Isas, the nine-year-olds, this morning, and then helping the Medicus team by learning how to set bones on a wooden human figure this afternoon. They want us all to know how to tend to cuts and scrapes and broken bones. After that, I am scheduled to spend time in the Seed Park, pruning and tending the flowering trees.

William1 should be with me. I swallow quietly and try to remember to breathe.

"I'm always busy, Regulus, you know that," I say. What is he playing at?

"Yes, you and William1 are always busy, aren't you?"

I stare at him. "Since you set the schedules for us, Regulus, yes, you know that we are. We are always busy." I have my chin set in the air, and I refuse to look away from him. I cannot imagine what is coming next. I simply refuse to raise the issue of what happened last night. I can only assume that since he knows everything, he must know that William1 walked through the door and is missing. Since Mother of William1 is in chains at my side, I think he must know.

But I will not be the one to raise it.

The Senate door opens behind us, and we all turn to look.

A boy walks into the room, accompanied by a Mother. It is William2. He's second-oldest boy after William1, and a friend to us both. He's pleasant, taller and slimmer than William1, with dark, curly hair and a quick smile. He enters the room, and Regulus summons him to join us.

"Miranda1, pleased to see you this fine morning," William2 says quietly, bowing to me. "And Mother of Miranda1," he adds, bowing to Mother. He does not acknowledge Mother of William1, who has shut her eyes.

I am about to greet him when Regulus says, "Welcome William1, we are pleased you could join us." I'm confused and look at William2, then my eyes slide to his armband.

He is wearing the deep red patch but with a silver "W1" embroidered upon it. His Mother has the same armband, deep red with a silver "W1."

Regulus watches us closely. "Say hello to William1, Miranda1. Where are your manners?" I consider Regulus. I look at William2, masquerading as my life-long friend William1, and I have a choice.

I can pretend that this boy is William1, bide my time, play along.

Or I can tell Regulus, tell everyone, that this is all a lie, and that there is a world Outside, and the real William1 is there now. I can tell them all that I will not play along with them.

But … I simply don't know what would happen then. I need more time to see what Regulus is planning.

I smile and bend my knee and bow my head. "Welcome, William1," I say calmly. "We must hurry to class. The Simons and Isas shall miss us." I know immediately that I shall never call him William1 out loud again. I shall always call him "William2" in my heart and mind and simply "William" if I must use his name aloud. A small act of defiance.

"You must go on your way then, Miranda1 and William1," Regulus says, staring at me, and I nod.

"Yes, we have chores to attend to," I say as haughtily as I can.

Then William2 and I leave the Senate together and hurry across the square and the common to the Teaching Hall. Two Mothers leave the building behind us, mine and the Mother of William2, wearing her false armband of "W1." I pretend all is well. I talk to William2 about the day ahead. I am an excellent actress, a liar, a brilliant pretender.

I have to be now.

I have seen what Regulus does to those who don't play along.

As we left the Senate, I dropped my satchel and for a second turned and saw Regulus descend the stairs. He stopped before the Mother in chains, the Mother of William1, then with a swift move, he reached deep into her chest.

He wrenched out her mechanical heart.

She slumped forward, and her metallic arms in chains hit the cold marble floor.

CLANG!

Regulus crushed the mechanical heart in his cold grip and threw the broken thing on the marble before he strode away. The true Mother of William1, the one I have known all my life, is dead.

Regulus just killed her.

I joined William2 before Regulus saw me watching him.

Although I know nothing of death and have never seen it before, I suddenly realize that more than anything, I want to live.

MANNFRED

Next day Grannie isn't feeling well, so we don't travel. Instead we stay in the courtyard, which feels safe enough, almost comforting. There are small busted houses all around us and the other family with Littluns.

People come by to swap with us. A woman who lives nearby brings water for a few fresh eggs from our hen. She's got a pump and a well near her house. A blacksmith comes and checks Nellie's loose horseshoe, which needs a shape and a nail. Grannie gives him a small knife from the Shiny Man, for his help. Another woman brings fresh herbs and carrots, which Grannie trades for some of her blue cloth. Grannie and this lady talk a long time, and it's like watching Grannie chat with our old neighbor back home. This courtyard has a friendly feel. There are pictures on the walls of the houses, like roosters and sunsets and a bird with a mighty blue fan-tail of feathers.

The pictures are faded, but you can still see them. They're made in what Grannie calls "tile." When I ask Grannie about the fan-tail bird, she says it's a picture of what was called a "peacock." I run my hand over the shape of the bird on the wall. The City has wonders, big and small. The shining dome with the lifted top has been in my head all morning. It's all I can think about.

Cranker and me laze all day, which is good. We fix up the cart a little, walk the horses, and rub them down. The Littluns play with the Littluns from the other family.

All in all, we're not so bad off for a family fleeing a sunken home.

The sky is beautiful all day, the beginning of spring. Back home at Grannie's, I know the big trees would be starting their leaves; even the mud might be greening with lichen and moss.

As night draws in, two lone travelers arrive and stop with us in the courtyard, a man on a horse with a pack, a woman with a cart. After dinner, when the Littluns are asleep and Grannie sits by her fire and smokes her pipe, she invites them to join us.

The woman says thankee, but no, and goes to sleep in her cart. But the man joins us.

His name is Briar. Jonatan Briar. He's youngish, solid-built, with a kind face and a deep voice. I'm taken by his black beard, the biggest I ever seen, even bigger than the Shiny Man's. He sits at our fire, and for a while he plays a strange tune on a sound pipe he calls a "recorder." We've heard music before, of course, Grannie sings to us, and once in a while a Music Man would visit us in the village and play drums and sing old songs. But I never seen or heard a recorder before. It makes me calm and quiet.

After a few songs, Jonatan Briar puts the recorder away in a pouch at his side. His pouch has his name tooled on it in big, rough letters: J. Briar.

Grannie tells him a little about us then, about how the Black Rain flooded out our home, and how we're going to stay with her brother on the other side of the City because they got room and land.

Jonatan Briar tells us that he grew up a long way from here, and that he's a traveler. He comes and goes often, since he's a stonemason by trade and good with sums. He tells us he helped rebuild some of the Olden Begones arches and standing walls in the great buildings in Oculum City.

"What's that? Oculum City?" Cranker pipes up, and Jonatan Briar looks surprised.

"That's this place. This city is Oculum City, though I suppose most people don't know that or forgot." I look over at Grannie, but she just shrugs.

"Well, what's it mean? Oculum? Funny word," Cranker demands.

"It means 'eye' in a long-dead language," Briar answers. "And an *oculus* is the open circular 'eye' at the top of very ancient domes."

"From the Olden Begones times?" I ask.

Jonatan Briar shakes his head and sighs. "Well, the Olden Begones used them, too. But they come from a time long before then, Mann."

He seems almost sad, so I ask him how far away he

came from, he smiles and says, "Weeks by boat, then as many again on horseback. I grew up on an island in a great northern sea, where educated men and women taught me reading and writing, mathematics, building, and something much more."

"What? What'd they teach you?" Cranker asks.

Briar's beard wags, and his eyes shine in the firelight. "Stories, Cranker. The great, old *stories*."

Grannie blows out a long breath of smoke, spies him, and says, "Tell us a story then, Jonatan Briar."

The big beard swings my way, and Jonatan says, "What kind of a story would you like? Mann? Cranker?" I been thinking all day about only one thing, the only thing I would want to hear a story about.

"Cranker and me saw the dome in the distance last night, and we watched it open. A huge corkscrew turned and turned and pushed the top up into the sky. It seems like Olden Begones magic. Do you have a story for that, Jonatan Briar?" The big man smiles and crinkles his eyes and nods, and says, yes, he does.

And so Jonatan Briar tells us his story he learned on an island in a northern sea, while we sit under the stars by the fire in an Olden Begones courtyard with a peacock picture on the walls.

Here's what he says: "Listen close, and I'll tell you the legend of Oculum City. This city. This is a story found in books that are kept for safekeeping in the library on the island where I'm from."

"What's *library*?" Cranker asks. I'm glad he asked, because I want to know, too.

"It's a building that houses many books and keeps knowledge. You'll pass a broken one here, along the road ahead, but it's empty now. There are hundreds of books in the library in my home. Imagine that! And every book holds a story, either a true one or a make-believe one. The one I'm going to tell is true, or so the librarians say, but you must decide for yourself."

"Grannie got a book by a man named Aesop," Cranker says, trying to sound wise.

Briar nods, thoughtful. "Those are ancient fables. Some stories last a long, long time, Cranker." Then he starts his story.

"A long time ago in the Olden Begones, before the Black Rain and when fruit trees bloomed, this was a vast city, roaring with life. Hundreds of thousands of people lived in this city, and they had the magic of kings. They had light without fire, they had water without wells, they had power that you could not see, and machines that went on four wheels across the land, but without horses.

"They had the power of the air and great machines that took flight. They could talk to each other over great distances, without pigeons or fire, but with the black boxes you see like an ocean at the side of roads. They rode in their machines, and sent their messages, and built their empire. Oculum City is only one of hundreds of cities like it across our world. People come from far away and tell us there are cities like this one in their lands, too."

Cranker and me look at each other and Cranker says, "Hundreds?"

Jonatan Briar nods. "Hundreds, maybe thousands, and most of them bigger than this one. In the city we're in now the people built a dome. They called it the Oculum City Dome. The same dome you saw opening the other night. It rose into the sky like a crystal mountain, and it was used for special days of ceremony, games, and for festivals and celebration. When the weather was fair, the top of the dome was raised by a simple mechanism, and it was a beautiful sight. The people of the city enjoyed the dome and used it for pleasure and entertainment.

"But as we all know, there was a price to their use of the light without fire and the power you could not see. The Black Rains came, the fevers came too, then the bees died off, the fruit and other crops began to fail." Grannie smokes her pipe, and me and Cranker sit and listen. It's always a sad thing to remember or talk about, when the Black Rains first came and the world changed forever. Grannie told us the rest of the story too when we were little, about the Dying Fever and other lesser fevers that came after, and the panic and fear and madness that took off most everyone in the end.

It was not something you talked about.

So no one really did, at least not very often. You

learned the stories when you were little, and that was enough. The early Black Rains brought terror and sickness, and terror and sickness brought collapse and mayhem, and mayhem brought the end of the mighty civilization. It brought the end of almost everything, along with the end of peaches and pears.

I stir the fire up with a stick and add another piece of wood.

Jonatan Briar goes on. "The people of the Olden Begones couldn't stop the Black Rain, though they tried. There was no magic they could think of that could save the bees, or the crops, or in the end, themselves.

"Some saw what was coming and went away and learned how to survive without the power you could not see. They learned how to grow hardy grains in dark soil, they learned how to raise sturdy goats and hens, how to make candles and clothes, and how to live in a different way from everything they knew before. Some also could survive the Dying Fever. They'd be sick but not dying sick. That's why you, me, and Grannie and these Littluns, why any of us are here: because some people went away and learned a new life. And survived sickness and hardship."

We all heard this part of the story before, too, how a very few clever people survived from the Olden Begones since they built tiny farms and greenhouses, learned new ways, and found crops that grew without bees in the dark soil after the Black Rain. They were also lucky or strong enough not to die from fever.

"In Oculum City the people knew they were doomed. They could not save themselves. But they *could* save their children, or some of them. So they made a magic, a kind of medicine that could put a child into a safe sleep for a long time. They gave the children strength in their bodies called 'immunity' that would protect them from illness, even from the fevers that killed. They created an army of simple helpers made of metal and leather who worked on the power of the sun and who could run the Oculum City Dome without guidance. Then they chose one thousand babies from the city and sealed them inside."

"Were they dead?" I ask. The thought of Lisle sealed inside the dome asleep for all time made me fearful.

Jonatan Briar shakes his head. "No, they used the medicine that would put a child to sleep. So not dead, just waiting to be woken."

"They's all asleep?" Cranker asks, doubtful. Briar nods.

"Yes. So the story goes. These thousand babies go to sleep, and the Oculum City Dome is sealed up, and outside the world changes forever with the Black Rain, illness, and mayhem. But inside the simple machines work away to keep the sleeping babies safe. Once every year, year in and year out for decades, then for ages and ages, the machines open the dome and test the air for a poison that made the Black Rain come. If the poison fell below dangerous levels for long enough, then the machines would start to wake the babies, fifty girls and fifty boys a year, until all one thousand babies awoke. Then the Olden Begones hoped their children would grow and one day start the mighty city all over again."

"How long would that take to wake them?" Cranker asks. He never was very good at his numbers.

"Mann?" Jonatan asks.

I sum it up in my head. So fifty boys and fifty girls, that's one hundred babies a year, until all one thousand was woke. "Once the first baby was woke ... ten years to wake them all?" I say, concentrating.

Jonatan nods. "Good math, Mann. You'd make master stonemason!" This makes me feel strange. I don't hear praise much. But something is bothering me.

"Couldn't they ever get out?" I ask. "Once they woke up?"

Jonatan winks at me. I think he thinks I'm smart. "Good question, Mann. What would be the point of a dome that you couldn't get out of? Why save all those children if they couldn't leave the dome when they were ready?"

"Why, they'd be nothing but prisoners," Cranker says. He wants Jonatan Briar to think he's smart, too. The big man shifts his weight and leans into the fire.

"That's so, Cranker. There's a story in one of the books in the library about a secret door for the children inside to discover when they were ready. But no one has ever found it, although no one has looked too hard, as far as I know."

Jonatan Briar comes closer to Cranker and me, and we both draw nearer.

"Along with the babies, the Olden Begones sealed up something else in the dome. Can you guess what?" I shrug, and Cranker shakes his head. Jonatan Briar pokes me in the arm.

"Seeds. Seeds that would grow trees, bushes and crops that bore fruit. Special hardy fruit trees and crops made to withstand the harsh new environment after the Black Rain. And they sealed up special, hardy new bees to do what's needed to make the fruit healthy. When the air was safe again, the machines would start the first crops in the dome. Along with the babies, they'd wake up the bees and the fruit trees."

We stare at him, silent and doubtful.

"What machines could do all that?" I ask after a silence.

"They were very smart in the Olden Begones."

"Not smart enough to save themselves," Grannie says. "Not smart enough to stop the Black Rain. Nor the fever." She was always one for pointing out the very truth of a thing.

We all sit quiet for a while, watching the fire, thinking about Jonatan's story.

"Is it true, though?" I ask. "About the babies and the machines ... and the fruit trees?"

Jonatan Briar doesn't answer me right away, when he does he sounds like he's not sure, like he's considering.

"I tell you, it was taught to me as a legend, but legends

can be true, Mann, or at least partly true. The men and women who taught me are smart, well-learned, and the keepers of the old knowledge. They spend all their lives reading about the Olden Begones. In their library they have ancient books and papers called 'magazines,' and even some very precious relics called 'newspapers' from long ago, in special dry vaults beneath thick glass so they don't age so quickly. They write out the stories they read in the books, magazines, and newspapers so that they aren't lost forever. They teach their children the stories from the Olden Begones so that we will travel into the world when we're grown and tell others. Tell you. My job is to keep the old stories alive."

"I thought your job was to build with stone and do sums," Cranker points out.

Briar laughs. "Well, yes, that too, Cranker. Stories don't make a living, and stone does."

"But if it's true, or partway true, wouldn't we know it? Wouldn't we see people in the dome? Wouldn't we know they were in there?" I can't get enough of this story. The sight of the golden dome glowing in the sunset last night as it opened will stay with me forever.

"The dome is thick, Mann. It's too thick to break through, and the old entrances from long ago have been blocked, and no one knows where to look for them, anyway. Besides, if they *are* in there, maybe the babies are all still asleep? People do talk about scaling the dome one day and climbing in through the open top, but frankly, we have bigger things to do first. And it's a long way up, and how would you do it? Besides, it's hard to get up close because of the piles of Olden Begones garbage, cars, trucks and buses ..."

"What's *cars, trucks and buses*?" Cranker asks.

"Oh, those are the wheeled carts, or the huge machines and the giant wagons with hundreds of seats. They carried many people at once in them. So it's difficult to get up close to the dome, and those who *do* get close only report seeing strange lights and phantoms through the glass."

"More Olden Begones magic?" I ask.

"Perhaps, Mann. Magic, or machines."

"What machines?" I ask again. This story has my head whirling and a thousand questions I want to ask, but Jonatan Briar laughs and stands up.

"That's all I can tell you. I do know that people say the Oculum City Dome is opening more regularly in recent years, so whatever mechanical devices are there are still in good working order."

"Do you think it's true? Are there children still alive in there?" I have to know what he thinks. He puts a huge hand on my shoulder.

"I only know the old stories as I was taught them, Mann. Now you know one of them, too. Tell everyone, tell the Littluns, tell the people you meet, keep it alive. It may mean something to someone one day. As for babies being woken and growing up into healthy children countless years later?" He considers and shakes his head. "I don't see how."

Then Jonatan Briar says goodnight and goes to sleep next to his horse. When I wake in the cold dawn the next morning, he's gone.

And all the Littluns are burning up and sick and coughing.

The Dying Fever is upon us.

MIRANDA1

William2 is with me in the classroom. We are helping the Simons and Isas with their numbers, and I am doing a terrible job of it. I am too distracted to make sense of what the children are asking me. A Sentry stands at the door, watching me. William2 sits at my side, pleasant, cheerful with the children who seek our help, but I simply cannot do this.

"William, I'm not feeling well, I must get some air," I say quietly. It's true enough. I have a terrible pain behind my eyes and in my chest. He has been very kind to me all morning, but he's uneasy. The children are calling him William1, but it's plain they are confused. They keep glancing at his armband with "W1" on it and looking at his face. Up until today, he has always been "William2" among us. They are nine-year-olds, not too young to notice this change.

"Yes, of course Miranda1." He hesitates. "Miranda," he corrects himself. If I am to be familiar and call him simply William, he should do the same with me. We are both playing a game.

"Shall I tell Teacher?" he asks. He is genuinely

concerned, a kind boy, and there is also something else in his warm eyes — worry, fear.

I shake my head. "No, that's not necessary. Perhaps I will sit alone, quietly? That's all I need."

"Of course. I can answer all the children's questions," he says. And then he rolls up his sleeves and begins to help the children gathered all around us.

I am sensing something else about the children, however. A few of them look at me curiously, sideways, with a question in their eyes. I don't know if they're curious about the arrival of a new William1 … or if it is something else.

I walk to the window and look toward the Seed Park, which is glorious now that our world is open. The apple trees sway gently, and the scent of their blossoms is almost overwhelming. Near the distant walnut tree I see Sentries — a dozen of them or more — at attention or milling around beneath it.

The door is well-guarded. There will be no getting near it now.

Usually I enjoy a day like this, with the open sky above and fruit trees in bloom.

But today everything has changed.

A young girl stands beside me. "Miranda1?" she asks quietly.

"Yes, Isa19?" I say, composing myself. Isa19 gives me a small, careful drawing. I gasp when I look at it: it is a very good likeness of my William1, the real one. It is far advanced for a nine-year-old, unless this child has an astonishing gift for art. I stare at her, shocked. What can it mean?

"I'm sorry," she says.

"Sorry?" I ask, confused.

"Yes, sorry about William …" Here she looks around and drops her voice, "I'm sorry about William1, your William."

"What do you mean?" I must look terrifying, because the child trembles but stands firm. She has some courage in her, this girl.

"I just mean, I'm sorry. I'm sorry that the first William1 … has died." She breathes this so low that I barely hear her. Then she turns and runs back to her seat.

Died? *Died?*

I look over at the Sentry, and I have to leave the room. Now. I brush past William2 and whisper in his ear that I must leave, then I grab my satchel and run past the Sentry, which wheels quickly behind me.

"Where is Miranda1 going?" it asks in its mechanical way. It reaches out and holds me in a steel grip. I pull my arm free.

"I must talk to Regulus," I say. "Now let me go." The Sentry allows me to leave the Teaching Hall but stays close behind me. I walk as quickly as I can across the common toward the Senate. I have no idea what I am going to say to Regulus when I get there.

I reach the square in front of the Senate, take a few steps, and stop. There is a new picture posted upon the signboard, where Regulus posts notices about the day; fruits available, market days, waking days, games, celebrations. I walk slowly forward, because there is a poster with a drawing of a face upon it.

It is William1's face. My William, the true William1. The child in Teaching Hall merely copied it, which is why her drawing was so skilled.

I stand before the signpost and read the headline below William1's image: "*Beloved William1, 13 years of age, dead of a fall, last night.*"

Below the headline is a short paragraph: "*William1, beloved by all, fell from the great black walnut tree in a forbidden evening meeting with Miranda1. We shall celebrate William1's life tomorrow night, at seven o'clock, in the square. All of Oculum must attend.*"

I swallow, but my throat is tight. I reach up to remove the poster, but the Sentry stops me.

"You killed William1," it says in a dull voice.

I turn and say fiercely, "You do not speak to me like that. I shall tell Toolman there is something wrong with your slow, mechanical brain if you breathe another word to me about William1." I say this with such anger that the Sentry wheels slightly backward.

William1's face on the signpost has awoken a fire in me.

Regulus is a murderer. He killed Mother of

William1 this morning.

He is a liar, since he is telling us that William1 *died*, the first death any of us has experienced, and that somehow I was involved. He is also toying with me, since we both know that William1 is not dead.

But more than that, the fire tells me something else: I must read the truth on the Map of Oculum, and I must find William1. I look up at the sky, the Arm stretched full-length toward the open air. The sun above shines down at my feet, upon the common, across the drawing of William1's face.

Clouds pass above Oculum.

And very slowly, an idea comes to me.

I cannot follow William1 through the door now that it is guarded so carefully, but there is another way out of Oculum.

And I shall take it tomorrow night.

WILLIAM1

The door opens only one way: outward.

I know this now.

I walked through the door and stared at the spot where it just closed behind me. But from Outside, there was no trace of it. The door was only visible from *inside* Oculum.

I ran to the wall, pressed my face against the glass, and looked into Oculum. Miranda1 stood where I just left her, but she was vague, shadowy. I banged upon the door and called her name. I could see her, but she didn't look like Miranda1 anymore. Instead, I saw a strange, wriggling figure rise and leap, distorted through the opaque wall. The Sentries were filmy, shifting shapes that moved like terrifying shadows beside her.

If I did not know what they were, I would not know that a girl stood there with Sentries. I would see only wavering, shimmering figures.

I would only see Fandoms.

The trees nearby were invisible. From Outside there was no trace of them. I fell to sit, my back against the door, or where the door once was. I peeked above me, but all around me was darkness. There were stars though, filling the sky, too many stars.

I trembled and shook.

I was alone. And shut out of the only world I had ever known.

I touched, again and again, the book in my cloak pocket. The book from my Mother: *For the Children of Oculum*. I read it over and over, and I had learned the truth about Oculum; it is a closed world and *we were not meant to stay inside it forever*! We were meant to leave, when we were ready. Without the book and the poem inside it, I would not have had the courage to go through the door, but sitting in the Outside that first night, it was little comfort.

I spent the first dark night with my back against the door. Strange, fearsome creatures with sharp noses and wicked teeth sniffed and hissed at me, and I threw whatever I could find to send them scattering. The next morning, though, came a transformation. The sun ascended into the sky, a shocking sight. Then the world grew rosy, and I could see, for the first time, where I was.

A new world.

Above me the great wall rose above my head, curving away, disappearing beyond my vision. The wall dug into the earth at my feet and ran to the left and right of me as far as I could see. The open space above me held the sun and the clouds in a bright blue sky. The sky went on and on, forever. It took a long time to calm myself and to look up without fear at the wide-open world.

I stood in a wasteland of rubble, wheeled metallic shapes, black boxes of all sizes, and more strange items that made no sense. I opened some of the boxes and found markings inside, letters, numbers, words: *Insert, Delete, Enter*. And other partial words, *PrtSc* or *PgUp*.

There were enormous machines in the wasteland as well, abandoned and broken. None was as big as the Oculum Arm, but they reminded me of Sentries, Mothers, or Nursies, since they had wheels and were made of metal. Many of the machines had broken windows and seats inside. I opened the door of one and sat in the seat behind a wheel. There was another seat to my right, and two more behind me, and strange instruments before me, more numbers and words I could not decipher: *radio, volume, speed, fuel*. I could read the words, but they meant nothing to me.

I supposed this was a kind of cart. These metal carts made the bulk of a solid wall all around. It was only where I stood, near the door, that the pile was lower, and I could see the bare, muddy earth.

For a while that first day, I banged upon the door with everything at hand, rocks, metal poles, trying to find reentry. But no matter how I tried, I could not get back into Oculum.

When night came again, I slept in one of the wheeled carts. The fearsome creatures returned when the sun fell, but again I threw rocks and the black boxes, whatever I could find, to make them run off. The foul things watched me from the wasteland in frightening numbers.

What a fool I was to leave Oculum so unprepared.

I needed fire, I needed shelter, I needed more food and water than the small amount I had with me. A handful of dried fruit, a small jug of water, and three peaches would not last long.

I could not stay in this place.

With the returning sun, I knew I had to leave. But if I were ever to return, I would need a trace of the door so that I could find it again. I picked up muck and dirt and drew an outline of the door where I knew it to be. When I had finished, I had made a mud copy of the real door that lay beneath. But a mud outline would only wash away with the next rain, I reasoned. I needed something more permanent.

So I took boxes from the piles all around me, and I stacked them up in a great, sturdy wall around the mud outline of the door. The odd, flat boxes with the strange words inside made good building blocks, so I used many of them, and rocks and more from the wasteland to build an outline of the door I knew to be there. I made the false door as strong as I could, tossing rocks at it to see if it would collapse.

When I had finished building my outline of the door, it looked strangely formidable, tall and thick and well above my head.

Then I took apart hundreds of the strange letters from the black boxes, breaking them out with a rock, and I wrote a message in the soil before the door in letters as long as my foot: *WILLIAM1 WAS HERE.*

I pressed my feet and hands deep into the mud, leaving my prints beside my name. And then, in a moment of pure vanity, I laid my muddied hands upon the pearled wall of my lost world. I left handprints, a muddy face print, and then finally with more mud I wrote: *W1's Door.*

The garbage outline of the door will hold for some time, and my name in letters will remain, too, but my message in mud will wash away with the first rains. Still, I made my mark; any wayfarers who are as lost as I am in this place will know that I was once here: a boy named William1.

It was past midday when I created my final act of vanity.

From the boxes and stones at my feet, I built a man. I gave my man of rubble a head, a body, arms, and legs. I crowned him King WILLIAM1 with broken letters from the black boxes. My image in the rubble stood as tall as I could reach, and I was surprised how well he looked. *This is my substitute,* I thought. This is my way home. If ever I return looking for the door, this man of rubble, made by my hand and crowned with my name, will point the way.

And now it's time to leave. I take one last look upon the door, and turn away from Oculum into the wasteland.

Before I go twenty paces, though, I stop. A creature covered in black hair waits on a pile of rubble ahead of me. It stands on four legs and has only one eye, the other shut and missing. It gently moves its back from side to side, and I think this creature means me no harm. It disappears, then reappears farther away in the rubble, looks at me again, then turns away. It wants me to follow. It must need water and food, and maybe it will show me water and food, too.

I turn away from the door, my message, my king of garbage, and set out through the rubble behind the one-eyed creature. My mission is simple now: find someone to help me free Miranda1 and the children of Oculum. I have the book of truth from Mother in my cloak, and as I walk, I recite the poem from the book, again and again:

We have left you,
The thousand chosen,
Kept you all safe here, at the fall.
There is a door,
And you must find it,
There is a door, within the wall.
Be the brave ones,
Then pass beyond it,
The Mothers shall rise, at the call.

MANNFRED

The coughing is terrible. It's awful to look at the Littluns like this, all red and covered in tiny dots that stand out on their skin, burned up with fever. One of them is too poorly to wake up.

I'm afraid for the Littluns. Lisle is still well enough, and no spots have turned up on her yet, but Grannie says they may, so there is nothing we can do for her until they do.

Grannie says it's not exactly like the Dying Fever; it's maybe one of the other lesser fevers, but it's too soon to tell. Whatever sickness, our Littluns caught it from the other cart of Littluns they been playing with. That family is all sick with it too, and the courtyard is filled with hot bodies laid out on sheets, burning up, or crying out, or whimpering. Or coughing. Or worse, lying dull and quiet and staring at the sky.

Cranker and me take all the eggs the hen laid and knock where people are living in between houses or in courtyards, and trade for water, just water, for our sick Littluns. One woman takes pity on us. She has plenty of Littluns in her own yard, a grannie herself. She gives us two whole goatskins of water from her well, enough for days. We thank her and tell her where Grannie is tending the sick, since she asks.

When we get back with the water, Grannie has two sacks for us. She pushes them into our hands then says we have to go now. The first of the Littluns has died, she says. Not one of ours, but one from the other family, and she don't want to lose her two grown boys. I never seen Grannie afraid in all my life, not 'til now.

So we got to go, not to come back for three days, Grannie says. I pack up my knife, my woolen sweater, and Grannie's sack has some hard bread and dried meat in it, and a FatRat skin full of water for each of us. She gives Cranker a flint for making fire, and then she does what she never does. Grannie leans in quick and gives me a kiss on the forehead, and one for Cranker, too.

Then she turns away to tend to one of the Littluns who is calling her.

It's hard to leave, but we do. It's midday, and we both know where we're headed. We got three days before we can return, and that's how long it will take us to get to the dome and back.

We set out through the rubble, away from the main road. Cranker has a piece of charcoal with him from the fire. I have one too, and we mark the corners and sides of buildings where we turn and twist away from Grannie's courtyard and all our Littluns. This is how we mark a trail back to them, since we don't know this place, and the piles of garbage all start to look the same. I put my name, MANN, big and bold, under roofs and along porches, so if it rains we can still see it, and Cranker adds bold arrows pointing back the way we come.

We pass through empty streets. The sliding-down buildings, the piles of bricks and garbage, and what Jonatan Briar calls cars and buses, make it hard going. Out here, away from the main streets into the City, no one clears the falling ancient houses, the piles of brick and glass. We pick our way, trying to find streets that are still passable. Sometimes we can. Sometimes we can't and have to climb over mountains of garbage and rocks and tumbled-down buildings. Sometimes we climb so high, we're on the same level as the tops of buildings, and we can look out over the busted City before us. It just goes on and on, like there's no end.

And as the day goes by, the dome gets closer and closer.

There are places, too, where people live in small families, or even a few families together in sturdy houses still standing. They remind me of our village back home, just a few houses built up between the bigger houses, surrounded by a river of garbage or cars or those big buses. Most people are nice enough to us when they see us, a few even curious and chat a bit.

I think how strange that me, Mann, a boy from nowhere, is standing knee-deep in the Olden Begones garbage, talking with Cranker to strangers about where we come from, who we are. I get used to it quick enough.

People are pretty interesting and pleasanter than I would have thought even a few days ago.

Only a few turned us away with rocks or called out to be off.

We want nothing from them, so we just hop it and get out of there.

And once we hear a loud laugh too close and freeze, then hide behind a pile of bricks. I almost shout when I see a boy with a shaved head leading three other people through the rubble.

"It's them, those thieves from the gate!" I whisper to Cranker, who frowns. His whole body is tense, and I know he's itching to fire his slingshot. I put my hand on his shoulder and shake my head. The slingshot stays in his belt, but he picks up a stone. I hold my breath, but the gang of thieves don't see us. They keep walking, and soon they're gone the other way.

"It's four against two," I say to Cranker, who spits in their direction when they're out of sight.

"They's not so tough, no match for us, Mann," he says, fierce.

"Come on, let's put some space between us," I answer, pulling Cranker to his feet. I don't say it, but how'd he know? How did Cranker know we'd see them again? Just more Cranker wisdom, I guess.

We make our way toward the dome as best we can. It's hard work, and by nightfall, the dome is closer, but we can't walk over the rubble at night. It's too dangerous.

So we stop in the shadow of the mighty dome that goes up and up and up farther than anything I could imagine. Now we're so close to it, it's like a mighty mountain, a miracle of glass and Olden Begones magic.

We find a covered front porch of an old house still standing and lay out two sleeping rolls that Grannie put in our sacks. We eat a little hard bread and a bite of dried meat. Cranker's been trying to shoot some FatRats, since we seen some, but these FatRats are smart and faster than the ones back home. He had no luck, so there's no fresh meat to roast.

But we're too excited to care much about food. We lie on the snug porch and look up at the giant dome nearby. It's too big to see the top now, but just knowing it's so close and so beautiful sends me to sleep with dreams of Olden Begones magic all night. Carts that go without horses, buses that carry one hundred people or more. I fall asleep wishing I asked Jonatan Briar what the tunnels underground were for in *Subway*, since I'm sure he would know.

The next morning we wake, and it's fine and clear. We walk, and our adventure is coming to an end. Soon I'll touch the dome I been dreaming about for days. But it won't be that simple, I start to see. We go through rougher ground, and the closer we get to the dome, the more garbage and bigger piles of rubble we walk through. It's slow going, dangerous and tiring.

When we finally get close, almost to the shining wall,

there are piles of overturned buses piled on top of each other, and great metal machines I couldn't say the point of, and slabs of the brick they make the roads out of with little pebbles in it. We get stuck in a huge pile of garbage, and Cranker almost twists his ankle. I pull him out, and we both sit and catch our breath. The sun is hot, and I stow my sweater in my sack then tie the sack back over my shoulder. We each take a sip of water from our FatRat skin.

"It don't look like we can get too much closer," Cranker finally says. We're disappointed, but neither of us wants to admit it.

"I don't want to go back yet, and we can't anyway. We got two more days." Cranker nods and wipes some sweat from the back of his neck.

"There has to be a way to get closer," I say, hopeful. "We just need to get up higher and ..." Cranker stops me. He puts his finger to his lips and draws out his slingshot. There's a soft noise over a ridge of bricks not far off. He loads his slingshot with a chunk of the road stone, draws it back, holds it steady.

"The thieves again?" I whisper. My heart drums in my chest.

A black dog head appears above the rubble, spies us, then disappears. It sees me, though. Cranker puts down his slingshot and looks at me, then says, "I'm jiggered if that ain't your one-eyed dog from back home, Mann!"

I'm just as shocked. He's right. It's the one-eyed dog

— it has to be him. There aren't that many dogs around, plus it's the same eye missing, but he's been scarce for a few days. I make Cranker stow his slingshot and promise not to shoot him, and he does, but I make him swear. Then I tell him that the dog's been shadowing me all the way since home. He woke me, and that's how I saved the mules the other day. Cranker seems impressed, so the dog is safe from his slingshot, at least for now.

Then we get up, and what else can we do?

We go over the rubble and follow the one-eyed dog.

MIRANDA1

I have spent the night and day quietly going about my business. Now that Regulus has told his lie, and the picture and announcement of William1's death is on the signpost on the common, everyone who passes me says they are very sorry to hear the news. They are almost breathless when they tell me, and I realize that we have so little news to share in our lives. Nothing momentous.

Never a death.

It seems to me that everyone is saddened, of course, but they are something else, too. Curious. Maybe even slightly excited by this strange new event.

A few older children, and some of the other Mirandas, even cry about the loss of William1. A small number seem so heartbroken that I realize I should seem more upset than I am, for their sake. So for the second time in my life, I lie. I go right along with Regulus. I manage to summon tears, just a few, when children and Mothers ask me what happened. I am demure, and sad, and shake my head to convey that I am too deeply upset to discuss it. No one doubts my tears, and no one accuses me of wrongdoing, even if Regulus did say that William1 died because of a forbidden meeting with me at the walnut tree.

No one seems to care about that part of the story, so if Regulus was hoping that I would be chastised by the community, he was wrong. The truth is, people seem genuinely moved by my plight; my William1 is dead. Death is an exotic idea for people who have never seen it before.

And of course, it is all lies.

I am a superb actress. I had no idea, and realize that I should have acted in some of Teacher's school plays over the years. I have a capacity for it that I never suspected.

But perhaps my talent is driven purely by terror at what I am about to do?

William1 has been gone for two days, and tonight is his death ceremony.

I will be ready.

This afternoon in Medicus Hall, a group of Mirandas and Williams, including William2 and I, are learning how to set bones again. It involves a great deal of linen bandages and wrapping of wooden human figures. I splint and wrap a broken forearm, a broken ankle, a broken wrist. William2 does the same.

When we leave Medicus Hall hours later, my satchel is bulging with rolls and rolls of used linen bandages, but no one thinks to question me about it. In fact, my new state of grief allows me all the freedom I need. No one wants to question me about anything.

I have to act quickly, and without fear.

I need another item. When William2 and I have our hour in the Seed Park, I find the nearest Treekeeper's hut, which is very close to the walnut tree. I tell William2 that I want to be alone, and he doesn't question me. I head toward the walnut tree, the place of William1's untimely death, and no one stops me. I can only guess this is because they assume I am in mourning, this sadness that happens after a death, and want to return to the scene of my dearest friend's demise. I try to look like I'm grieving; I keep my head bowed, my eyes damp.

Even the Sentries leave me alone, and there are many of them, standing rigidly row upon row near the rose trellis. Near the door.

When no one is watching, I slip into the Treekeeper's hut and find a rope ladder, the longest one they have. This is the ladder the twelve-year-olds use when they climb to the top of the mighty walnut in their annual coming-of-age rite. This ladder is thin as a whip, lightweight, strong. The one and only time I have used it, I almost fell to my death from the walnut, but I try not to think about this. I slip the ladder over my shoulder and under my cloak. It is no bulkier than my suspiciously bulging satchel. A pair of short-handled pruning shears hangs on the wall, and I grab them and stick them in my cloak pocket. A package of apple seeds sits beside them, and I put those in my other pocket. I had not intended to steal the shears or seeds, but they seem too useful to dismiss.

After the Seed Park, I walk back to my house. I look oddly misshapen, but again no one questions me. No one would dare. The Sentry follows me closely, so I pretend to be weeping. I stop in front of William1's house, which now has a small cluster of flowers and pictures laid on the walk and at the base of the stairs. Children and their Mothers have been dropping off small messages and items at his house all day.

Grief is odd. We have learned about it in Teaching Hall but never felt it. This reaching out with pictures and messages is strange and new, and I don't quite understand it, but I pretend to. I walk up the steps of William1's house and try to look majestic and weepy. Children and Mothers move out of my way and whisper, "Sorry, dear Miranda1," as I walk past. Then I step into William1's house, a place I have never been allowed unaccompanied before. The Sentry tries to follow me, but I stop.

"I ... I need a few moments alone in his house, please." The Sentry is puzzled but also slightly alarmed at my tears, and so it allows me into the house alone.

It is dark in William1's house, and it already feels abandoned.

I scan the mess. If she were alive, the Mother of William1 would not allow it. I think of her for a moment, slumped over in chains, take a deep breath, then move deeper into the empty room. There are some of William1's papers, an unfinished plate of fruit, and there it is! I see William's hand-drawn Map of Oculum spread out on the table. The map is detailed, clever, with a close-up of the Oculum Arm. I rush, snatch it up, and turn it over. There is William1's handwriting, tiny and exact, as he said. I scan quickly and see a poem, then a tiny note, in the bottom right-hand corner, addressed to me.

M1
Learn the poem by heart.
The Mothers will help us.
The Sentries will not.
W1

I read this frustratingly short note several times. Then I read the poem:

We have left you,
The thousand chosen,
Kept you all safe here, at the fall.
There is a door,
And you must find it,
There is a door, within the wall.
Be the brave ones,
Then pass beyond it,
The Mothers shall rise, at the call.

I puzzle over William's letter and the poem. They don't tell me much that I don't already know. I would never expect a Sentry to do anything but detain and annoy me, so the fact that they will not help us is no surprise. And the poem tells me very little other than that the Mothers *shall rise*. But what does that mean? Simply that my Mother would rise every morning to wake, feed, and dress me? The poem does say that we must be brave and go through the door, though, which is interesting.

But even this is small comfort, and I'm about to curse William1 for being so vague when the door opens and the Sentry says, "Hurry, Miranda1," in its dull voice. I quickly roll up the map and hide it in my long cloak pocket.

"I will take exactly the amount of time that I require," I snap, and the Sentry's head disappears. The front door shuts.

William1 was working on this map for as long as I can remember. He was a very good artist. No, he *is* a very good artist, and he is alive and well, and I have to go and find him. I'm appalled that the mystery of death has already seduced me into using the past tense when thinking of him.

William1 is alive, and he will be looking for me, wherever he is. I turn to the stairs and walk up into his empty bedroom. William's pants and shirts are all over the floor, and his shoes. His bed is unmade. I quickly sort through the closet. There is one set of pants that are shorter than the others, and I try them on under my frock and cloak. They fit well, if a bit loose, so I take one of his leather belts and strap them so they fit snugly. Then I take two of his smaller shirts, shirts from last year that his Mother had not yet sent to the younger children. I wear both shirts under my frock and cloak. I realize I look extremely bloated under my cloak, but I will have to hope that no one inspects me too closely.

I shall just have to weep and wail if they do to alarm them.

I leave William's house, looking downcast and weepy, and again no one questions me or stops me. I sweep through the crowd of children and Mothers and head along the streets to my house. The Sentry is close behind me, but it stops at the bottom stair and turns to face the street when we arrive. I shut the door behind me and hurry up to my room.

Mother comes from her closet when she hears me and taps quietly at my door. I ask her not to come in, and she timidly asks if she can get me food.

"Yes, Mother dear. Please get me half a dozen of last year's apples and peaches. And a bowl of dried cherries from last year's harvest. I am quite famished. And a sealed jug of water." Mother wheels away to the kitchen to gather this food for me, an unusually large amount, but she doesn't question me. I do have a good appetite, but I've never eaten half a dozen apples in one sitting before. Or peaches. I can only hope she puts it down to grief, although everything I have read about it says that the opposite happens. The bereaved tends not to eat. Perhaps Mother does not know this.

I remove the bandages from the satchel, the rope ladder, William's clothes, the pruning shears, the small bag of apple seeds. I unroll the bandages one by one, and I realize why I took the shears. Slowly, carefully, I begin to cut the linen bandages in half. I need a long, long, long rope for what I am going to do. Impossibly long.

When Mother comes with my food, I ask her to leave it at the door, and she doesn't question me. I hear her wheels gently roll into her closet. There is just a tiny sound; already she is squeaking after her visit to Toolman. She is getting old and worn out, I think sadly. But I need her to squeak. I need to know where she is.

I work feverishly, since I have only a few hours to prepare. At seven o'clock tonight I must join the others on the common to mourn the death of my dear, departed friend.

MANNFRED

The dog slips away over the rubble, and we follow. He keeps just out of range of Cranker's slingshot, and every once in a while we don't see him and I worry that we lost him. But right about then he turns up over the top of an overturned bus or a huge busted chunk of road and looks at me, then we head his way again until he disappears.

I don't know where he's taking us, but it's clear we got to follow.

After about an hour, we're within a slingshot of the dome. Up close, it's like a giant pearl stuck in the busted City. We know the top is open, because we seen it open two nights ago, and we haven't heard it close yet, but this close we can't see it. It's too far above us, straight up.

The dome shoots into the sky, a beautiful, magic pearl.

The dog is nowhere in sight, but he brought us to a place where the rubble is thinner, and there's a kind of pathway where you can walk safer and down. Cranker and me head down into this pile, when he stops me.

He points.

The dog is lying at the feet of a figure. There's a *man* in the rubble. Or really, a man MADE of rubble. Someone made a man out of garbage, a pretty good likeness too. He has a head, a torso, arms, and legs. He's tall, over our heads, and he wears a crown of letters from the black boxes. As soon as the dog sees that we found the man made of Olden Begones garbage, he takes off at a run. He slinks over a distant pile of garbage, then another farther away, smaller and smaller, but don't look back. I can't help thinking he brought us where he wanted.

To this crowned figure of garbage.

"Dog's weird," Cranker says. Then he tries to read the crown.

"W ... Will ..." he starts.

"William1, it says." I hurry him along. I'm better at letters than Cranker. He looks at me with wonder.

"What the heck's William1?" In all the piles of garbage and rubble and destruction we seen in the City, it's all been random. Broken signposts, busted half-words on buses or big boards with words and faded letters on them for stuff we don't understand. Like giant ladies with long curls and something called "hair color." Or stuff for teeth, called "toothpaste." Or men and women with huge faces talking about something called "insurance." These images are broke, half there and buried deep, faded so much that we only spy a face or word down in the garbage piles below us. We walk over them and under them, and at first we read them, but after a while they're so common that we stop. It's just more Olden Begones junk.

But this figure is a thing made here, the first sign of a living human hand in the waste. Someone made him and crowned him William1.

It's strange.

Who made it? And why?

We look at each other, but Cranker is braver than me. Or sometimes I wonder if he's just got less imagination. Anyway, he smiles, since there's an adventure here, he can tell. Then he heads down into the well of garbage ahead of me. I hear him shout, and I run to catch up.

There's the dome, right there. We walk up and we both touch it and grin at each other. It's warm from the sunlight, and we lean against it and laugh. We bang against it, we peer into it, but we can't see inside.

Cranker walks a little out of sight. "I'll be jiggered!" he shouts.

I run up.

There's a door built against the wall!

It's marked out in black boxes!

On the ground in front of the door, it says in the same letters as the crowned garbage man, "William1 was here." There's deep, muddy footprints and handprints beside it, and Cranker and me put our feet into the prints. Mine are bigger, Cranker's are about the same.

There's muddy handprints all over the glass, and foot-prints, even a face outlined in mud. Cranker and me add a tiny bit of water to the dried mud and make our own muddy handprints, footprints, and faceprints alongside. I take out the charcoal, and I write on the dome: MANN WAS HERE.

There's words in mud on the door, too: W1's DOOR.

Cranker looks at me. "You know, this mud message couldn't be too old. The last Black Rain would wash it off." I nod. He's right. He's not great with letters and numbers, but Cranker is plenty smart. Wise, Grannie calls him.

"Not more than a week old," he adds. "Or less."

"So who's William1 then? This W1?" I ask. Cranker thinks.

"Well, we know he's about like us, with feet and hands the same size. His name must be William1." Cranker points at the message on the ground. "And he made his own image, up there." He points back the way of the garbage king. "And this here *says* it's a door, W1's Door, outlined in garbage."

"It's a doorway," I say. I get a little shot of nerves up my back, through my neck, up to my hair. I can see Cranker feels the same way.

"Doors was meant to be opened, right, Mann?" He grins at me, and we both start booting and hammering on that door like no tomorrow. Truth is, except for the outline of black boxes, the word "door" and a little mud, there's no door that we can see. It's just more dome glass, pearly and hard as nails, reaching into the sky.

We throw chunks of busted-up road or whatever we can find at the sweet spot between the black box outline of a door, but there's no dent. Not a mark. We keep at it. We scare up a load of FatRats, who scurry off, surprised.

Soon, though, we tire. Then Cranker gets an idea. He says to think of a blacksmith, the man who fixed Nellie's horseshoe a few nights back. The blacksmith used two pieces of metal to make the horseshoe fit right, one he held and one he banged upon.

"But he heated it up," I add. "We can't."

"No, not heat it up. But throw two rocks at the same place at the same time," he says, and I see what he means. He gets me to draw a circle in charcoal in the middle of the doorway, and we spend the next hour trying to hit the circle at the same time with two chunks of rock.

Which does nothing.

Finally, Cranker gets mad, takes out his slingshot, and starts pinging huge rocks, as big as he can shoot, at the door. Then he picks up a piece of metal and shoots that. I find a good spot above the door on a flat pile of rock, and I rain down metal and chunks of road, right at the same spot.

Then it happens. Pure luck, or stupid timing, or just the right amount of both a shot piece of metal and my giant boulder ramming it home, but suddenly we hear a tiny creak, and we both stop and run forward.

Somehow, there's the piece of metal that Cranker shot stuck in the glass in the center of the door. It's not very big, but it's stuck all right. He shot the hard, raggedy piece of shiny metal, and in perfect timing, my boulder rammed it home.

We look at it, proud for a minute. We slap hands and do a little dance around the door. We did it! The piece of metal is sliced right into the door, about the length of my finger. We're impressed that we managed this. Can't fault us for trying. We bang on the sliver of metal with rocks and sticks for a while, but that does nothing. After a while, the stuck metal piece seems like enough, as close to opening the door as we'll get.

And as we stare into the glass, feeling proud and brave, a weird figure appears on the other side of the door.

I jump back. It's slithery, and monster-looking, and scary as anything I ever seen.

"What's that?" I shout, and Cranker comes to look.

"Save us, it's a ghost!" Cranker shouts, and we both run off a little. The strange, ghost-thing looks monstrous on the other side of the glass. It floats and shimmers, stretches and shrinks, and two huge staring eyes leap out of it.

We grab our packs and run farther off, but when we look back, the ghostly figure is gone.

We eat quick, a little of Grannie's dried meat and a few bites of bread. I'm thirsty as anything but only allow myself two small mouthfuls of water, enough to wet my tongue. The sun is raging down now, it's midafternoon, and we should go back the way we come and find shelter for the night. Plus I don't want to stay here another second with the ghost thing on the other side of the glass.

Before we go, Cranker goes back to the door, picks up another huge rock, and rams it into the stuck metal piece a few times. Then he calls me over.

"Look," he says, pointing. I don't want to get near the door again, but I swallow my fear and go look. There's a crack in the glass, a small one, starting around our stuck piece of metal. It runs upward and out about a hand's-breadth. I raise my eyebrows.

"We did that? Made that crack?"

Cranker nods. "We did. Come on, let's go."

We take one last look at the door, at our piece of shiny metal lodged there, then we turn away. There's no more phantom face on the other side, peering back at us. I think about that face, the stuck piece of metal, and that crack all the way back to the porch we slept in the night before.

I don't say it to Cranker, but I think that crack we made in the door is deep, deeper than it looked at first glance.

MIRANDA1

I am sweating, cloaked and bundled as I am. I stand at the front of the square in the place of honor at the head of almost one thousand Oculum dwellers. William2 stands beside me.

All Mothers are with us, and there are Sentries everywhere, some I've never seen before, a style that seems outdated, standing along the edge of the crowd.

Oculum is open, and the early twilight is beautiful. It is a gorgeous night.

And I am a bulky, sweating liar. I have my cloak done tightly over my clothes — or William1's pants and shirt — and over my bulging satchel and the Treekeeper's rope ladder and linen bandages. I also have my first satchel under my cloak, the satchel I used when I was a younger child, and it is bulging with apples, peaches, dried cherries, and a sealed jar of water. One pocket has garden shears in it, the other a bag of apple seeds, and inside my cloak, in the long pocket, is William1's Map of Oculum. It's all I have of my friend until I find him again.

And I will find him.

I must look enormously lumpy and strange to everyone, but thankfully, no one has come too close to me. They are giving me space in my grief, or perhaps they are simply too afraid to come near.

All but Mother, who has clucked and whirred and taken care of me all day. We left the house together, and she did not ask what I was hiding under my cloak, although she surely noticed. Instead she took me by the arm, and we walked together to the square. She's standing beside me now, next to Mother of William2 and William2 himself. They both look uncomfortable wearing the false red "W1" on their armbands.

The Senate clock gently chimes seven bells, and Regulus strides onto the stage that has been hastily built for this occasion. Behind him is an enormous picture of William1, the real one, the likeness from the poster that was hanging on the signpost in the common. I suddenly have a longing to see William1, and the thought of what I am about to do makes my knees weak.

"Are you all right, Miranda my darling?" Mother whispers.

"Yes, Mother, I'm fine," I lie.

Regulus takes his place on the stage, and there is polite applause, and he begins to speak. He does have fine elocution and a deep, commanding voice.

"My dear children of Oculum. Today is a terribly sad day, for today we must say goodbye to our oldest, dearest boy. William1 has died." He stops for effect, and the crowd murmurs quietly. *Yes, yes,* they say. *William1 has died.* The children nod and look at each other and at their Mothers.

I stare straight ahead.

Regulus goes on. "Now, we do not understand death, or what it is to have died, but I tell you today that William1 will not die, if we remember him as he lived: with our respect. He will live on in our hearts." *Yes, yes,* the crowd murmurs, *he will live on in our hearts.*

I take a deep breath and begin my bid for freedom.

I step forward, then take two more steps, then slowly, regally, I walk up the stairs to share the stage with Regulus. He has not asked me to do this, but I am grieving, I am not to be denied. I hope that Regulus will feel as everyone else has for two days and not question me.

He is surprised as I step onto the stage, but he smiles and turns back to the crowd.

"Ah, dear Miranda1 has come to share her grief with us, how wonderful." I am about to speak when I realize that Mother has followed me up the ramp and onto the stage.

I was not expecting this, but I will have to improvise.

"Thank you, Regulus," I say calmly, looking over the sea of children, with their trusting faces turned toward me.

"Children of Oculum," I say in my most mature Miranda1 voice. "I am here to tell you ... that

WILLIAM1 IS NOT DEAD! HE HAS ESCAPED OCULUM THROUGH A DOOR IN THE SEED PARK! HE IS OUTSIDE, AND OUTSIDE IS REAL!" I scream this as loudly as I can, then I turn and run off the stage and disappear into the Senate.

There is a roar behind me, and I can hear the almost one thousand voices cry out. I run across the Atrium and leap up the stairs to Regulus's chair. I only have a moment, and I hear Regulus yell at everyone to be quiet, and then the Senate doors bang open behind me.

Regulus and Mother burst into the Atrium. Regulus runs on his metallic feet, but Mother is faster on wheels and spins like a whirlwind in my direction. I have already clambered up onto Regulus's chair at the bottom of the Oculum Arm. I reach as high as I can and pull myself up onto the first platform, over the giant bolts and to the base of the mighty machine.

Up, up!

Everything is much, much bigger from up here, and the ground is much, much farther away. I gulp and step onto the first rim of the Arm reaching into the sky and immediately slip. I quickly climb back on, but my shoes slip off again.

I will have to climb barefoot.

Regulus runs up the stairs, Mother speeds up the ramp, and both reach Regulus's chair. I take off my shoes and throw first one shoe and then the other as hard as I can at Regulus. Both shoes hit him in the head, which surprises him, and he stops to look up at me. Mother is at his side, staring up at me as well.

The Senate door bangs open again, and a flood of Sentries wheel into the room.

"STOP!" Regulus commands, and the Sentries all freeze, although I think he was talking to me. Without my shoes, I climb the Arm quickly. I climb like I would climb a ladder, hand, foot, hand, foot, and the edges of the massive corkscrew give me enough space to grip. I'm already looking down on them all. I try not to think how far I have to go.

Regulus walks to his chair, then to the base of the Arm. And I forgot one thing about Regulus; unlike all the other caregivers and minders in Oculum, *Regulus alone has legs and feet*. He is not on wheels. He is about to climb after me — I can almost not say this next part for it nearly makes me fall — when my own dear Mother shoots forward and grabs Regulus in her metallic grip.

For a moment he's surprised, and Mother doesn't hesitate. She plunges her other arm deep into his chest, and with a wrenching shriek of metal, she tears out his mechanical heart. She crushes his heart to dust beneath her wheels.

Regulus slumps to the ground.

Regulus is dead!

Mother and I look at each other, and sweetly, so sweetly she whispers, "Goodbye, Miranda my darling." Then my dear Mother reaches into her own chest and wrenches out her own mechanical heart. She slumps over Regulus, and in the next second their two bodies are swarmed by an army of Sentries.

It will be impossible to get close to the Arm with their bodies there. My Mother has given me time to climb!

"Goodbye, Mother dear," I whisper. My eyes fill with tears, but I have no time for shock or grief.

Mother said that she did not think love was so very evil after William1 told Regulus that we were in love. I know now that Mother understood love. And she wanted me to climb to the sky.

I grit my teeth and climb. I cannot fall, I cannot fail, I must make it to the top of the Arm.

The Sentries stare up at me, but none can climb to catch me. Some begin to slowly move the tangled bulk of Mother and Regulus aside. I am well above them now, hand over hand, climbing the mechanical Arm. I reach the top of the Senate building and climb out into the open. The gathered children on the common see me and call out. I can hear their voices, small already from my height. "Look! LOOK! It is Miranda1!"

They sound eager, astonished, and I can only hope it is because they want to see me succeed, not because they want to see me fall.

Surely this is the most exciting day of their lives. First a death, and now this. The escape of Miranda1: my bid for freedom.

I climb, aware that every eye is upon me. I have been

climbing for five minutes, and I am already a quarter of the way to the top of the Arm. How like a spider I must look, I think, climbing her web. I can hear children below calling to me, or to each other, but most of them are silent.

Perhaps they are holding their breath?

Then … the great Arm begins to turn. I gasp and hold on tight for a moment as the machine lurches to life beneath me. This is the closest I have come to falling. Why didn't I think of this! Of course the Sentries below me would turn on the machine and close Oculum. Without Regulus, the Sentries have taken longer to think of it than he would have, but that is a small comfort.

I do not have much time.

The Sentries have set the mechanism in motion. I halt for a moment, look down, and have one life-long question answered. I see now how the Arm works: Sentries wheel it open and closed. They spin in tight circles along the track at the bottom, attached to the Arm with a heavy leather belt. Sentries whirl around the base of the Arm below me, turning it slowly closed. My Mother and Regulus lie in a heap, cleared to the side of the track.

I put on a burst of speed. I am halfway to the top, but I can see the great lid, the top of Oculum, already beginning to slowly drop into place.

NO! I am not going to fail now!

I climb, and climb, and climb. I think my arms are going to break. The children below call me, but I can't hear their words, just a low murmuring shout of noise and my name punctuating the wave: Miranda1! Miranda1!

The creaking Arm turns more quickly, and I have to climb faster to keep from falling off, but I keep going. If William1 can leave this place by walking through a door, then I can leave by climbing into the sky, although I think William1 had the easier job of it.

I'm just a few body lengths from the top now, but the Arm drops the great lid of Oculum lower and lower. There is just enough room for me to squeeze through the opening ... and I do it! I clamber to the very top of the Arm, and out onto the curved wall before the Arm drops and seals my world shut. Quickly, I take the stolen ladder out from under my cloak and snap the large hooks into place on the opening.

I cling to the ladder and close my eyes. I'm very close to the moving Arm. Just a slip would send me under it, where I'd be crushed to death and stuck like a butterfly beneath glass, until the next time Oculum was opened.

I hang on, and then with a sigh, the great Arm shuts Oculum tight, catching the edge of my ladder in the seal.

I open one eye and quickly shut it.

I am Outside. There is a terrifying, wide-open space all around me and a dizzying openness below.

Night is coming. And I am clinging to a ladder, attached to the top of the only world I have ever known.

I take a deep breath. And another.

Then I save myself.

I kick the Treekeeper's ladder over the edge, and it clatters open. I hear it bang below me over the curved, smooth wall, farther, farther, then it stops. I can only hope it goes a long way down. I have climbed the walnut tree with this ladder, it is very, very long ... but can it possibly be long enough to reach the ground? The linen bandages that I cut and tied to the bottom of the ladder are on the last rung. I can only hope they will hold me.

I peek for a moment, take a quick look out at the world below me, and gasp. It goes on and on as far as I can see, and I feel dizzy. Sick. My heart hammers in my chest, and I have to lean my forehead against the wall and close my eyes. I think of Mother, I think of William, and I am calmer, but I can't look out at the vast world again. Not yet.

I lower myself onto the ladder and test its strength.

The ladder holds. Slowly, rung by rung, I begin my curved descent from the top of my world, down to whatever fate waits in the unknown, below.

MANNFRED

Cranker and me head away from the dome and walk back the way we come, following our charcoal marks through the garbage piles. There's an arrow here on an upside down bus, my name there on a slab of broke road brick. We walk for hours, thinking about what we seen.

Who was William1? We think about him and his door. About the mighty dome and the crack we made. As night comes on and we get around the great curve of the dome, there's a noise off in the bricks, away from our path.

The one-eyed dog pops his head up over the rubble and spies me. He runs onto an upside down bus in front of us and barks. Awful bold of him. I never heard him bark before. Cranker spies him, too.

"What's his problem, do you suppose?" Cranker says. I shrug.

"Maybe he wants something?"

Cranker looks up at the sky. The sun is going down. "Hey, the dome is closing!"

He's right. We both stand and watch as the dome lid starts to close. It seems faster closing than when it opened a few nights ago. I want to watch it close, but the dog pops his head up, a little farther this time, and barks again, wags his tail down low, then disappears.

"I'm going to follow him," I say.

"We got one more day before we's supposed to go back to Grannie. Time for another adventure," Cranker says with a grin.

We leave our old path, making more marks with the charcoal along the new route. It's easier going; there's less garbage as we get farther from the dome. The overturned buses and cars turn into flat chunks of broken road, and soon we walk through houses again, but we're on the other side of the center of the City, the opposite side from where Grannie is.

The dog pops his head up now and then to make sure we're following. The sun dips lower in the sky then sets. Suddenly the dog does a YIP! YIP! We see him head back the way we just come.

"What the jigger's wrong with him now?" Cranker says. He's about to flare into a foul mood when I stop him. There ahead, near where the dog took off, there's something lying in the road.

A body.

The person is slumped in a long cloak, and four people stand around, looking down. The gang of thieves from the gates! I can see the shaved-head leader. Cranker ducks behind a house, and I follow. They don't see us.

I peek around the house, and it's a boy on the ground.

I can see his face now. He's got ginger hair. He's awake, but he's hurt. His foot is in a funny angle, like it's broke. He looks up at the faces above him, and he says something, but I can't make it out.

He doesn't look afraid, though.

The shaved-head thief says, "Water? Why'd we share water with you?" Then he spits at the road. I hear the rest of the gang growl and rumble. They shift a little.

Cranker says, quiet, "Mann, look at his arm." The boy on the ground has a red armband under his cloak. It says "W1" on it, plain as day.

"W1?" I whisper. Cranker nods. "William1? Must be the same boy from the door," Cranker says, a little awed. "Or kin, anyway."

"We got to do something," I say, but Cranker is already working. He builds in the rubble behind me, lifting rocks, placing them, lifting more, fast and sure. In a moment I see it's a body he's making, like the man of rubble crowned "William1" back at the dome. He places everything just right, and Cranker's garbage man shapes up quick.

"What you doing?" I whisper.

"Givin' us a chance," he says without looking up.

I peek around the house again, and the thieves bully William1 on the ground. But he seems brave. I hear him say, "Take it," then he hands over a book from inside his cloak, but the thieves don't want it. They leaf through it without looking, sniff it, tear out pages into little shreds, crumple them, and laugh and mock. Then they toss the ruined book on the road, a few torn pages blow along and away. William1 watches it fall but doesn't speak.

The thieves could take whatever they want from him, but they're having too much fun to hurry. One of the girls tugs at William1's cloak and shrieks. She found something.

She takes a water jug out of his pocket and upends it. Empty. But a glass jug, not broke, is valuable. She slips it into her coat and eyes William1's other pockets.

"We got to help him," I whisper to Cranker, who is still working fast behind me. I want to help William1, but I got a whittling knife and no skill as a fighter. No stomach for it, either.

Cranker finishes his man of rubble and lights a small fire, quick. There's plenty of wood to burn at hand. He uses the flint Grannie gave him, and the spark flares up and the flames catch. He adds another small pile of wood. Soon the thieves are going to notice us.

The flames flicker behind the garbage figure, and then I see what Cranker is doing: the flickering image of a tall man appears on the road beside the house. Cranker made a shadow figure, from rubble and fire, that looks just like a man.

"Now it's three against four. Go, step out, call them, Mann," Cranker says, shoving me. I got no time to ask what he thinks he's doing. I stumble out onto the road, and all eyes turn toward me. I stand as tall as I can.

"Hey, it's that big baby-lovin' fool from the gates!" one of the gang calls. I move into the road, and I see that the shadow of the man of rubble looks like a big man is standing behind me. The shadow figure flares out into the road and up onto the side of a house.

I take a deep breath.

"What do you want with William1?" I call out. I see William1 look at me in surprise. He don't know me. I don't know him. But I put my feet in his muddy foot-prints. I left my mark same place as he did at the door. I seen his image crowned in the rubble.

I know him, where he's been, well enough.

The shaved-head leader turns toward me. He takes a step, then another. He's got that toothless grin that makes me shudder. But I stand my ground.

"What the jigger are you doing here?" he shouts. "And where's t'other one? The short one?"

Cranker steps out from the house with his slingshot loaded and aimed. The thieves all got sticks, bricks, but a slingshot is rare, and Cranker's is new. And he's deadly. Even if they don't know that, he looks deadly. Fiercer than anyone else standing there, anyway. A few of them step back, just a little.

"First one of you thieving beggars moves is first to lose an eye!" Cranker snarls. He's curled like a bow, a tight little spring, and I fought him all my life. He's never been above biting. Or spitting. He'd be worth two of them in a fight, I bet. Me, though, they'd have no trouble with. I got my knife in my hand, but I alone know it's only ever been used to make a baby soother.

The fire behind the house rages now, sends our third man flickering across the road. A few of the thieves look at it, nervous. If I didn't know it was just fire and garbage, I'd be a little nervous, too. Looks awful big. But the leader has his doubts.

"It's just two against four, far as I can see," Shaved-Head says, taking a step closer.

We all stare at each other. Cranker's arm starts to shake from holding the heavy piece of rubber back to his ear.

"Which eye you want to lose?" Cranker spits back.

I can't see any way to end this that won't let blood. William1 has pushed himself to stand up but can't put weight on his foot.

"It's four against four," he says evenly. And then a thief shoves him, and he sprawls back onto the ground. They all laugh. He won't cry out, I notice.

Stay down, I think.

Then it happens.

YIP! YIP! A speeding black shadow whips out of the darkness and leaps into the group of thieves, snarling and snapping.

The one-eyed dog! He grabs onto Shaved-Head, tugs his arm, growling and fierce. Then another dog, one I never seen before, walks out of the darkness behind us. It's a huge mutt, gray and shaggy, and stands tall as my hip. It steps between me and Cranker, head down, teeth-bared, chest rumbling.

The thieves all spy the dog behind me then turn and run down the road. I see one fall, then cry out, a girl I think by the shriek, and run off holding an arm. The dogs chase them, worrying the thieves into the darkness.

I hear another squeal and shout, then nothing.

"Stay gone!" Cranker snarls, lowering the slingshot. We trot over to William1, who's standing on one foot.

"We seen your door," Cranker says. "Said W1 on it."

"He's Cranker. I'm Mann. You William1?" I ask. The boy nods.

"Yes, I'm William1. So you saw my door? It's still standing then. Thank you for saving me." William1 bends to pick up the ruined book on the road, but he can't reach it easily and winces, so I get it and hand it to him. He opens it, but all the pages are ripped out, tore up, blown away. He puts the ruined book back into his cloak.

"Do you have any water?" he asks. His voice is awful raspy.

I hand him my FatRat skin, he takes a sip. Then another. He's wearing a fine black cloak, black pants, and a black shirt. He has a leather bag over his shoulder. He's rich, he must be with such fine clothes. He's about our age. He's got the same amount of fuzzy hair on his chin as Cranker, the same boy-man voice. He points at the house beside Cranker's fire, which is burning lower.

The house has a sound front porch.

"Let's go by the fire. I have to sit down." Me and Cranker each hold him under an arm, and we help him hobble over to the porch.

"Nice man of garbage," William1 says, looking at Cranker's work. He laughs a little, an easy laugh, and I like him. But I can see he's nothing like Cranker and me. He's had a softer life than us, for one thing, I can tell by his long, fine hands. Plus he seems older than us put together, but he's not older — it's just the way he walks and talks, like he's used to being in charge. Cranker tends the fire, and we share some of our hard bread with William1. Cranker heads out for a few minutes then comes back with two dead FatRats, and we skin them and set them to roast on the fire.

Then we lay out our sleeping rolls and doze while dinner cooks. William1 wraps himself in his cloak and groans as he sets out his leg. Cranker and me don't say it, but he needs help. The only person I know could help him is Grannie.

We talk a little, easier and easier with each other. I want to ask him all about his door, where he's from, but I'm not used to new people. I start slow.

"How'd you hurt your foot?"

"Nothing very interesting, I'm afraid. I twisted it in the garbage pile trying to outrun those — thieving beggars did you call them? — then limped as far as I could, looking for help. Again, thank you to you and your creatures for saving me."

"You're easy pickings, that's true enough," Cranker grunts. William1 draws his cloak closer around him.

"They're not our creatures, the dogs. I mean the one-eyed dog been tailing us since back home, but that other gray monster I never seen before. We come from a little village, just ten houses, three days from the gates by cart," I say. I'm all chatty. William1 looks at me.

"You're the first people I've talked to out here, other than the thieves, and that wasn't exactly a civilized conversation. I have so many questions to ask you. But first, can you tell me where we are?" It's an odd question, and I shrug. "We're in the garbage piles of Oculum City, like everyone else," I say.

He's about to say something when Cranker cuts in. "Dinner's ready."

William1 falls back, silent. He seems exhausted, but his eyes are watchful. He's hungry, the way he eyes the food. The FatRats are cooked, so we slice them up and offer William1 his share. He tastes it, then spits it out.

"How can you eat this?" he says. He reaches into his bag and takes out a ball. It's light pink and orange, like a sunset. I never seen one like it before.

"What's that?" I ask.

William1 holds the ball to his nose and breathes deep. He closes his eyes. "It's a small piece of home," he says, sad.

"Does it have a name?" Cranker asks, chewing on a hank of FatRat and spitting a bone out into his hand.

William1 looks at us funny and frowns. "It's a peach, of course," he says. I stop chewing and stare at him. Cranker chokes on his mouthful of FatRat and spits it out.

"A ... *peach*?" I whisper.

Cranker looks at me, worried.

What seemed like a normal boy a moment ago just turned into a crazy boy, we're both thinking. And we're stuck with him, since we saved him and his bad foot.

What do we do now?

MIRANDA1

The last part is the hardest. I make it to the bottom of the rope ladder, but there is still much more space beneath me. With shaking hands, I undo the linen bandages and let them flutter below me, one end tied to the last rung of the ladder. There are strips and strips of bandages; they filled my bedroom floor, but it seems ridiculous now, here in the Outside.

I have to trust my life to linen bandages.

I wrap the rope-bandage across my back and hold it against my body, under my arms. I plant my bare feet on the wall, and I slowly let the bandage run through my left hand, then under my right arm. The Treekeepers have shown us this technique for descending a large tree.

The sun is going down, and the curved wall beneath my bare feet feels warm. I wonder if anyone can see me from inside Oculum. What do I look like? A strange Fandom spider wriggling down the world. Or maybe the Sentries have shut everyone up inside their homes, forbidding them to look? What's happening now that I have escaped with everyone watching? The children must be very afraid. They watched me escape through the top of our world, and now they know that William1 isn't dead.

I slowly walk backward down the curved wall, one foot, another foot, lower and lower. The ground slowly gets closer, and I peek out over this new world. There are houses, broken down and fallen over, as far as I can see. Smoke rises in a few places.

Are there people out here other than William1? A terrifying thought, but there must be.

There is no Oculum wall above me for the first time in my life. I can't scream in fright or give in to fear of the openness all around me. I have no choice but to be brave. If I die, at least it will be out here, in the Outside. Where William1 is.

I get to the end of the linen bandages, but it is still the height of my house to a landing spot. There are piles of rock and rubble below me, and I have no shoes. I dangle for a while, wondering what to do next.

My cloak.

I adore my cloak; of all my clothing it's the most dear and useful to me. Mother made it for me when I was four, when I first entered her house, and she let it out each year as I grew. It's hard to think of sacrificing it, but there's no other choice. I must cut up my cloak.

Mother would want me to, I realize. She would want me to live. Otherwise, why did she kill Regulus and sacrifice herself so that I could get away? I tie myself securely with the bandage rope and then wriggle out of my cloak.

I cut it with the pruning shears then tie the strips together and one end to the last linen bandage.

Then I descend the final distance, land, and roll on a flat piece of rubble. I'm bruised, I cut my leg, and banged my knees, but I'm unharmed. I look back the way I came. The curved wall of Oculum rises, up, up, up, above me, lost in sky. I can't see the rope ladder at all from here, just linen strips and my cloak, in shreds.

Thank you, Mother dear, for your handiwork.

I slump to the rock and lean against the wall.

It's unfathomable what I've done. It's ludicrous, crazy. I suddenly start to shake with exhaustion and fear. I can't move from this spot. I eat an apple, keep the core in my satchel, and take a sip of water from the water jug. Then I lean back and watch the sun disappear into the ground at the edge of the world, a strange and frightening sight. Darkness comes.

Where am I? And what have I done?

I lost the pruning shears after the final cut. They slipped out of my hand and into the rubble below, gone forever. And on the last tear of the cloak, William's map fluttered out across the ruined world like a bird. It floated a long way before it dropped on the ground.

The apple seeds are still safe, though. They're warm and solid against my waist.

It's a long and horrible first night outside my world. Foul, long-nosed creatures slip out of the rubble, hiss, and nip at each other, then at me. I throw rocks at them when their eyes glint in the moonlight. As I huddle upon the rock, I think of Jake47, Isa19, William2, and all the others, and I know only one thing for certain: I must find William1 and return to Oculum, even though we are both as banished from our world now as anyone ever could be.

Who will tell the children of Oculum the truth about Outside? William and I are the only ones who know.

Slowly the sky grows pink, and I watch the sun reappear on the opposite side of its sinking. I was too scared in my descent yesterday to really look at the world all around me, but now I do.

This world is ruined. The houses are fallen, the larger buildings too, and there is only destruction and garbage as far as I can see. It may have been beautiful once, though, judging by the color of the sky and the few trees that hold fast in the rubble.

There is no movement, no people. There is nothing alive, other than the long-nosed, hissing creatures that appear and disappear in the shadows.

I look down at my bare feet — how I wish I hadn't thrown my shoes at Regulus! — then I tear strips from the bottom of William's shirt and fashion shoes. I shoulder my satchels and pull a long, sturdy, wooden staff from the rubble. I slap it on the rock and sweep it through the air over my head.

It will do.

I take in the beautiful sky. It's strange and frightening

to have so much space above me, but I know now that this is how it should be. This is Outside, and it is the truth.

I turn away from Oculum and start across the wasteland to search for William1.

It's treacherous, and every step I take has to be careful and sure. All is silent but for my own breathing, my footfalls upon the rock and garbage, through the brick and glass and machines that I can't fathom. I see no one, hear nothing.

And then after a few hours ...

... a sound!

It floats on the air, and I cannot name it. It's not a voice. It's not a machine. It's just sweet and comforting, and it calls me. I creep cautiously past a fallen house. I don't know this sound.

And I stop.

Around the corner of the house stands a beast on four legs. It's much taller than I am, with a powerful back and chest, a fine head with a long fall of hair.

A man sits at the feet of this creature.

I know he is a man; Mother has taught me that William1 and all the other boys of Oculum will grow into men, but I had no idea what that meant until now. I've never seen a man before. The man has hair on his face like William1's, although much filled out. He is bigger across the shoulders than my friend, as well, and taller.

The man holds a stick in his mouth. He breathes into it … and this is what makes the sound, this stick and his breath! It is sweet and lovely, astonishing. I crouch and listen. The sound tugs at me, makes me want to move my arms, my feet, my hips, but I don't know how to approach, or if I would be safe.

I'm afraid.

The sound stops. The man puts the sound-maker stick into a pouch at his side, and I see letters on the pouch: J. Briar. A name?

J. Briar stands, brushes off his legs, and climbs onto the back of the beast, who is willing. The creature moves carefully through the rubble with heavy feet, and I watch as the man and beast disappear.

I have seen my first person in the world Outside.

He moves through the fallen houses and streets, and I follow, but the legs of his beast are much longer than mine, and soon he is gone.

I walk on and on over rubble and more broken houses. It's hot, difficult walking, and despite the cloth shoes my feet suffer, then start to bleed. I have no idea where to go to find William, but I decide that if I see anyone else, I will speak to them. Except for J. Briar, however, I see no one.

Then, in the wreckage of this world, a word peeks from the wall of a standing house: MANN. It's char-coaled on a wall, and there's a pointing arrow beneath. There's another "Mann" written again on a wall nearby, and another arrow. Someone has written this, left this word and this arrow, and I consider: should I trust it? But I have no other guide, no other sign of life, and so I see that I must. I stumble along, catching glimpses of *Mann* and the arrows, as I follow the path on my bleeding feet.

Then, in late afternoon, I come across my second person in this world.

I watch for a moment, leaning on my staff, astonished.

This person stands over many small children who are laid out on the ground. The children are ill, I can see that immediately. They cough or stare and lie still. The person moves between them, muttering. Then she looks up at me, and I gasp.

A woman. I know the word but again, I've never seen one. Other than J. Briar a few hours ago, I've never seen anyone older than me. I did not truly understand it.

As soon as she sees me, the woman runs toward me. Her hair is gray and flies all over her face. She's missing a tooth at the front of her mouth, and her face is not smooth like mine. She dashes to me and clutches me with a surprisingly strong hand. I draw back in fear.

"Girl! What do you want here? Who are you?" She's ferocious, shouting in my face, but I push her away.

"Please, I'm Miranda1. I've followed a trail to this place. I've followed Mann." At the last word, the woman raises her eyebrows and looks me up and down.

"You can't stay here, Miranda1. You must go." She

sees my bleeding feet, though, and clucks. I immediately think of Mother with a rush of sadness.

"I'm looking for my friend. Can you help me?" I ask, and I must be pitiful, for the woman bows her head and turns to a cart with two beasts attached to it. I understand now: these are beasts of burden, horses. J. Briar had one. I've seen the words in the WillBook, just never in life.

She rummages for a moment then returns to me with a pair of boots and a piece of food. She shoves both at me.

"Boots and bread, best I can do for you, girl. Now go! And if you find Mann, you tell him that Grannie says there's still fever among the Littluns and to stay away." Then the woman turns from me and dismisses me as thoroughly as if I was never there. A child whimpers in its fever, and she bends to soothe it. Another calls her name, and she soothes that one too, and wipes a brow, offers a sip of water, touches a hot forehead as she creeps among the sick.

I lean on my staff and watch and cannot stop it. A tear drops. And another.

Grannie, she called herself. And she reminds me in every possible way of my own dear Mother, gone forever.

Soon, though, I turn away, since she has told me to go. I strap on the boots, which fit well, then put the food to my lips. She called it bread. I've never had anything like this. It's chewy and hard but softens in my mouth.

I walk away from Grannie and her sick Littluns, as she called them.

I head into the coming darkness, alone, but in my mind I see Grannie bending over her sick children, and I can think of only one thing. It comes to me again and again: *Grannie loves them.*

MANNFRED

It's hot, even after the sun set. Me and Cranker been cursing and sweating for hours, and we drank all the water ages ago.

We carry William1 in his cape between us, and it's slow work. It was his idea, but it's heavy lifting for me and Cranker. He's not fit to walk, and his foot is huge, but we think it's not broke, just strained. We're almost back to Grannie's courtyard, and we got this boy with us. This amazing boy. I cannot wait to see Grannie's face when we come home and show her what we found. This miraculous boy and his even bigger miracle of a fuzzy, round, honey-from-the-sky peach.

Because I know now that *peaches are real.*

After William1 showed us his peach last night, we had no choice. Crazy or not, he held it out to us, and we had to do something, so Cranker took it with a look at me, and smelled it. I did the same. Then he licked it, then we each took a tiny piece between our teeth, and I almost cried. I never seen Cranker look so astonished, and we ate that peach with William1 in that porch, and we woke to some kind of new life. A life of Olden

Begones with miracles like peaches.

We all felt like kings. Cranker, he swore each time he took his turn with a tiny bite. But it was swearing that seemed almost loving, making that peach a blessed thing. We took an hour to eat it between us, and to lick the pit, and then our fingers.

Not one of us stopped smiling all night.

William1 was feeling fitter then, and he told us the most amazing story about his life inside that dome. I still can't imagine it's true. If we hadn't seen his door, his footprints, I think we would have a harder time believing him. But it must be true, and it sounds a lot like the story Jonatan Briar told us, too, about the babies waking up and the machines inside the Oculum City Dome. So here's the strange boy.

And more magical, here's the peach.

We carry William1 between us, over the piles of rubble and past the busted up houses, and we listen to his story and we tell him ours, about Black Rain (which he knows about) and the Olden Begones (which he doesn't). And about the now, and our place, and how there are no fruit or bees in this land, which makes him sad. He has questions, more than we can answer. He's a smart fellow, like no one I ever met. Except maybe Jonatan Briar.

Then I tell William1 about Jonatan Briar, about his books and his library folks, and about his story of Oculum City Dome. William1 says he remembers most of what he read in his ruined book and could write it all down again for Jonatan Briar, if he ever got the chance. This seems to cheer him some.

So now we're almost back to Grannie, but tired out and sore. Hungry, too. The one-eyed dog and the gray monster been shadowing us, ahead and behind, just wispy ideas of dogs, all day. But then the one-eyed dog runs past with something in his mouth. He drops it, makes sure I see it, and runs off. I know the dog well enough by now to see that I should pick it up. We lay William1 down on some flat road, and I walk over and see it's a paper.

It's a drawing, like nothing I ever seen, but I can read the heading: *Map of Oculum*. It's got houses and names like "Medicus Hall" and "Oculum Senate" on it. And lots of little houses with colors, letters, and numbers on them, like William1's armband says "W1" and the like. Plus there's a close-up drawing of a huge machine, like a corkscrew, reaching to the sky. I take it over to William1.

"What is it?" he asks, reaching.

"I don't know, but it looks like something from your place," I say, handing it over. He looks shocked when he sees it. He starts to gasp and splutter. Finally he says, "I cannot imagine how this got here. It's mine, from my house. It's my map. I've been working on it for years. It's like a bird dropped it from the sky."

Cranker and me don't know what to make of it, none

of us do, so William1 just tucks the map into a smart pocket he got in his cloak and says no more about it. Although he does seem worried about how that one-eyed dog found it. I'm beginning to think there's something weird about that dog.

We walk on for hours, long past dark, then past dinner, following our charcoal marks on the walls and porches until finally we get to the courtyard and stagger in proud with our fine surprise in a cloak ... and it's the saddest thing.

Grannie falls upon us. She's blubbering and clutching us like I never seen. Cranker and me set William1 down and try to calm her. A few of our Littluns come over and touch us, all afraid.

Then Grannie blubbers more, and we get the idea: most of our Littluns are dead and buried! Most of them are gone of the fever. The other family lost all of theirs, though, and they're gone away. The courtyard is empty except for Grannie and the last of our Littluns.

I sit and hold my head in my hands, and Cranker puts his hand on Grannie's head, and the three Littluns that are left to us come and sit beside me and lean against me. William1 limps over to us, and he can see how sad we are. He takes the three Littluns aside with a gentle smile and shows them a magic trick. He takes a pebble, hides it in his hand, waves his other hand over it, and when he opens his hand again, the pebble is gone. The Littluns take to him and watch, struck dumb. They don't even know this boy, and they already like him. One day, when I'm not so miserable, I hope he'll teach me the magic of the pebble trick.

Grannie never been like this before, crying and weeping and carrying on. Cranker and me take her and help her lay down in the cart, and she's all heart-broke and sobbing. She hands me Lisle, who smiles when she sees me, and I can't help but smile back. I'm so glad that Lisle is not took, too.

"The fever took them! My boys, my sweet little boys!" Grannie grabs at Cranker, and he sits beside her and talks to her and calms her, and he stays 'til she sleeps.

"You keep the baby. She's yours now, Mann. I don't want her," she says as she falls asleep.

"No, Grannie," I say. "Lisle needs you."

Grannie shakes her head. "No, she don't. I kill Littluns. I let them all die," she says, then starts on a new sobbing. I want to point out that it was fever, not her, and there's three of them still, not to mention Lisle is fine, and me and Cranker, too. But Cranker waves me off, and I know he'll take care of Grannie. So I give Lisle a sip of water and some mushy cooked grains I find, and she just burbles at me and grins and smiles and tugs at my shirt. I can smell I got to change a nappy, too, which I do. I did it before enough before we left.

I'm awful sad that we lost all those Littluns. They deserved to live. But I got a smiling baby girl in my arms. Sorry as I am, I'm glad to be looking down at that face.

The last three Littluns are struck by William1, who tells them a story, then another and another. He says they're from something called the WillBook, the seed of all thought in his world. Then William1 holds out something the Littluns never seen, or imagined could ever be, that catches the firelight and makes them all stare with the magic of it. The scent of William1's last peach drifts through the air to me, and it's so beautiful, I could almost cry. Then, with a sudden longing for something lost, something I never felt before, I do.

It's a long night, and after Grannie falls asleep with the Littluns, me and Cranker and William1 sit around the fire. We talk for hours, me holding Lisle in the blue sling, who sleeps like a dove under my arm, and we ask William1 questions, and he answers, then he asks us, and we answer. He's determined to get back to the dome and to his friend Miranda1, 'course he can't for a long while with his foot as it is. There's too much to discuss, so we go slow, a lifetime to talk about between the three of us, and we got to start at the beginning.

When Grannie wakes in the morning, she's fit again. We start to pack up camp, we got two days more of travel ahead of us, and while Cranker and me pack, she tends to William1. She has him sit up in the cart and wraps his ankle in special strips of cloth she cut for him. She also dug an old crutch out of the back of the cart, which is strange since I never seen such a thing before, but Grannie is full of surprises.

"You're a fine Medicus. I want to take you with me when I go," William1 says to Grannie, and she spies him. I'm not sure what Grannie makes of William1, the boy from inside Oculum City Dome. She seems a little wary of him and not over interested in his stories. She did sigh when he held out his last peach to her after she wrapped his foot, though, and smelled it, then looked away, like she didn't trust it. Maybe when she gets to know William1, she'll allow herself a taste. He put it back in his bag for her, for later, he says.

"You can't walk far, boy. Hobbling's all you can do for now. Where would you go?" Grannie says.

"I intend to walk back to Oculum — to the Oculum City Dome, as you call it — and find Miranda1 as soon as I am able." Grannie snaps up her head and stares at him.

"Who?" She gets close and peers into his face. William1 is seated in the cart, and I lift a Littlun in, listening. We're almost ready to go.

"M-Miranda1," he says, a little scared, since Grannie seems so fierce. "My friend."

"What she look like?" Grannie demands, and Cranker and me both stop what we're doing to watch. Something's up. William1 describes his friend, and Grannie's eyes get wide.

"She was here! That girl, that Miranda1, she was here, just hours before you came!"

"She was here?" William1 looks frantic. I lay a hand

on him to keep him from jumping out of the cart. He seems already to have forgot about his foot. "What did she say? What was she doing here? HOW was she here? You must tell me everything!"

Grannie can see William1 is too worked up, so she sighs and puts a hand on his shoulder.

"She's healthy. Her feet was bloodied, walking on shreds of cloth, so I gave her boots. And bread. Then I sent her off, because of the fever."

William1 stares at her.

"Then she might not be far off," I say. "If she was here not too long before us."

"We could find her, maybe," Cranker offers.

William1 jumps up, then winces and sits down. He nods. "Yes, yes, you must find her! Then bring her to me!" He's frantic, so Grannie looks at us with a tilt of her head, thinking. The three Littluns are tucked up in blankets in the cart with our one hen and all our worldly goods.

"Cranker, Mann, you willing to find this girl?" Grannie asks. We both nod.

Grannie decides. "You can go, and find us again on the main road in a few days. But we got something to do first." She calls to Nellie and Nancy, and the horses start a slow plod, out of the courtyard and back onto the main road. People are about already, and Cranker and me walk beside the cart. I got Lisle in the sling under my arm, and she's cooing and giggling at me all the way.

I have to be careful and watch the road, not the baby. It's a good thing when she falls asleep.

Soon, Grannie stops the cart and climbs down with a bundle. "Mann," she calls, handing the bundle to me, and I follow her. We walk down a short lane through two busted houses and into a yard. Another Grannie, about the same age as mine, comes out of the house. She wipes her hand on her apron and comes across to us. I realize this is the Grannie who gave us the two goatskins of water when our Littluns were sick. Grannie takes the bundle from me and hands it to the woman.

"For you, sister. All washed and mended. I lost Littluns to fever this week. May their boots and jackets serve yours through the years."

The two Grannies hug, and the other one says, "Go with strength, sister," and my Grannie says the same back. First time I ever seen Grannie so gentle with a stranger. We walk away, and that Grannie stands and waves. Quite a few Littluns clutch her skirt and watch us with big eyes as we leave them behind.

We take the cart a little farther along the road, and then Grannie stops and takes us to a heap of stones under a tree. There is no bare earth here, but it's a cemetery right enough. There are sticks with bright flags on them, all over this space, and under each small heap of rocks is a Littlun, ours and plenty of others, buried for all time. We bow our heads and Grannie says, "Goodbye, my boys. I woulda loved you 'til you was grown, and then some." Cranker says he's sorry for bullying them so often, and all I can say is goodbye. I'm too choked to say more.

William1 watches, sad. Grannie kneels beside each grave for a while, and we wait. A breeze blows the bare branches of the only tree in the place.

"I've never seen death," William1 says.

"You ain't?" Cranker asks. "That's a surprise. It's about all we got sometimes."

William1 shakes his head. "No, no one has ever died in Oculum." This is just more strangeness of his, as far as we can tell. How can you be from somewhere and never seen death?

"Well, you never seen death, and we never seen a peach before, so now we're even," I say.

Grannie joins us. Her tears are dry, she looks like Grannie again. She reaches into the cart and hands me and Cranker two sacks, again with supplies, bread, water.

"Go, find Miranda1, bring her back," Grannie says. "Find us on the road, we'll go slow," she says, and William1 gives me and Cranker a handshake each.

"Thank you," he says, a little choked himself. He reaches into his cloak and pulls out the Map of Oculum. He pulls out a feather quill and a stopper from a tiny bottle, then dips the quill in the ink. I watch over his shoulder as he writes on the back of the map: *Miranda, this is Mann and Cranker. They will help you find me. Come as fast as you can. William1*

"Good writing," I say, impressed, and William1 shrugs.

"We can all read and write in Oculum." Then he passes Cranker the map. "You must give her this, when you find her, to prove to her that you know me. She'll understand. Please, don't lose it," he says. *You should give it to me, then*, I think. Cranker takes the map, sticks it in his sack careful enough. I pass Lisle back to Grannie and miss her against my shoulder right away. But Cranker and me got a job out in the rubble.

We say our goodbyes and head back out into the broken-down City to find Miranda1.

MIRANDA1

I wander all night. The boots save my feet, and I stumble and push myself to keep on my way. The small moon is up, so I am not in darkness. Everywhere is bathed in silvery light. There are no more people, though, no one but me.

As the moon crosses the sky, I stagger, and soon I'm too tired to move. I know it's still hours from the return of the sun, so I sit against one of the few trees. I did not mean to sleep, but a moment later, it seems, I wake. There's a soft, warm body beside me, and I'm so surprised that I yell.

The body beside me leaps to its feet — all four of them — then runs out of my reach and looks at me. In the moonlight, I can see that it's dark, covered in fur, and one eye is missing. But the one good eye peering at me is intelligent. The creature gently sways its back from side to side, a peaceful motion, and I do not think it means to harm me.

"Do you have a name?" I ask, and the creature tilts its head to listen. How like Mother it seems for a moment!

"My name is Miranda1," I say. It looks at me, then out of the darkness quietly steps another creature like it, but gray and much bigger. The two creatures wait patiently, looking at me, gently swaying their backs together. Everything about them seems friendly, but they are waiting for something.

"I'll call you Ariel," I say to the smaller one without the eye. "And you I'll call Caliban," I say to the huge gray one. These are names from the story Teacher has read us from the WillBook, about the girl with my name, the story that I've never read to the end. Ariel and Caliban both wiggle their backs like they agree. We look at each other a moment longer, then as one, both creatures hear something in the darkness, and they vanish. But for some reason, I don't think they've abandoned me.

I walk farther, the moon sinks and the sky grows pink again ...

... and I find my third person in this world.

It's a girl, clutching her arm and crying softly. She sits in the road, and I walk up to her. After talking to Grannie, I assume she can understand me.

"Why do you cry?" I ask, and she whips around to look at me, afraid.

"Shove off!" she shouts, and I'm surprised, but I've seen this before in younger children when they're frightened. They yell at you. Although this girl seems my age or older.

"Are you hurt?" I ask, and the girl drops her head and sniffles. "Is it your arm?" I ask, slowly advancing. "I can look at it, maybe I can help? I can set bones." She still doesn't answer me, although she shoots me a quick glance.

"I'm Miranda1," I say, as though it may help. The girl cradles her hurt arm, and I creep a little closer, crouch, and hold out my hand. As gently as I can, I take her arm and prod like Medicus taught us. I assess. No bones broken.

"Can you make a fist?" I ask, and she can. "Can you squeeze my fingers?" I ask, and she does, although it's a very weak grip.

"You've sprained your wrist, I think. Nothing is broken. I need a bandage. Do you have one?" She looks at me.

"A *what*?"

"A strip of cloth? Or linen?" The girl just stares at me, so I tear another strip off the bottom of William1's shirt, suddenly thankful that it was far too long for me. I carefully take her arm and tie the bandage in place, then I fashion a sling for her and set her arm in it.

"Don't use it for seven days, then only for a few hours a day for another seven. It should heal completely."

I help the girl stand up, and she whispers, "Thank you." Then three people come out from around the side of a house, and the girl scampers over to them. One boy has a shaved head, and he stares at me, and says, "Who the jigger are you?" He's a little old to be missing his front teeth, but he spits this out at me.

"I'm Miranda1." I hold my staff and look at the four

people, about my age, two boys, two girls. They look underfed, rough, sad. The girl shows them her arm, and they look at me with suspicion, but their malice fades.

"You a healer?" the boy with the shaved head asks.

"No. I know how to set bones and treat sprains, though." The boy wants to say more to me, but suddenly the group grows uneasy and moves away, back toward the house. They disappear around it without a goodbye. When I turn around, Caliban and Ariel stand behind me like Sentries.

"They don't like you two. I wonder why?" The creatures dip their heads and trot ahead of me, one on either side. I'm about to continue on my way ...

"Miranda1!"

I whirl around, and there behind a house, two boys step out from the rubble, one huge, one short, much like the dogs. The bigger boy raises his hand in hello.

"Miranda1, we got a message for you," the short one calls.

"From William1," the big one adds. I run toward them and catch them both in an embrace. I don't care who they are.

"I am found."

MANNFRED

The hot sun beats down. Miranda1 marches ahead of me and Cranker, the dogs at either side of her, leading us through the piles of garbage around the dome. We lost the argument. We're going back to William1's door.

I learn something important today: Miranda1's got a will of steel. We told her who we were, that Grannie sent us, and showed her the Map of Oculum with William1's note. Then we said he was with Grannie, but hard as we tried, we couldn't make her come with us back to them on the road. Not even after I point out he wrote, "Come as fast as you can."

"He's safe?" she asked. We nod. "But he's hurt his foot?" We nod again.

"Then he can't help with what we need to do, and I'll find him afterward. Come on." Then she walks away, and there's nothing for it but for us to follow. Cranker and me shoot each other a look, but we both know we can't return to William1 and Grannie without her now she's found, so we fall in step behind. But truth is, I'm awed by her. Cranker, too. We'd follow her anyway.

With our charcoal marks all over, and the two dogs,

we set out for that door in the dome. We walk through the hot day for hours, then in late afternoon we turn down into that weird ditch between all the cars and buses. There's the garbage man, crowned William1, pointing the way.

The dogs run ahead, but Miranda1 stops at the man of garbage. She looks close up and then reaches and runs her hand across the face, the name "William1" in the crown. I see her smile, first time all day.

We walk a little farther, and there's the door.

But the door is broke!

It's busted wide open! Miranda1 stops at the door and puts her hand into the open space. She looks at us, amazed.

Cranker rushes up and looks. "Look what we did, Mann! Our piece of metal brought down the door!"

"Shhh," I say. "Quiet yourself, Cranker." I want to whisper. Something here feels strange. It's true, somehow the door is open and smashed. Could it be our doing? Our crack that spread?

"You did this?" Miranda1 asks.

I shrug. "Maybe. When we were here a few days ago, we stuck a piece of metal into the glass." She raises an eyebrow but turns back to the door. A shred of glass hangs over the busted door, and before I can stop him, Cranker whips a rock, and the glass falls. Above the door there's a web of thick cracks, running straight up. Cranker whips another heavy rock.

BANG!

"Cranker! Cut it out!" I shout, but he lets fly with more rocks. This time, there's a creak and a whine, and a big crack shoots farther above the open door. It's like watching one of Grannie's hen's eggs crack in boiling water.

"Stop it!" I shout and grab his arm. "You want to bring the whole thing down on us?" And there's no denying it: the cracks fan out, slow and even, and start spidering above the door. We both hold our breath, watching. The cracks run and run, then stop. We eye the dome, me a little worried and Cranker just about wild with excitement.

A bigger crack starts to moan, and run along again, bit by bit. I can't stand the thought of walking through the door now. There's nothing about the cracks that make me feel good.

Miranda1 pays no attention. She is through the open door and disappears into the gloomy dome. She sweeps past me, shifts her packs, hoists her staff, and I know that danger or no, I will follow her anywhere. Me and Cranker step through the wrecked door into Oculum City Dome behind her, into the world of Miranda1 and William1. The two dogs run ahead, sniffing and lurking like master thieves.

As soon as we step through the door, it's dark and quiet. There's a smell in here, like a too-closed space, but with lots of green plants. It reminds me of Grannie's greenhouse, back home, after it's been closed for days.

The dome is high over our heads, the space is filled with trees, and I can see buildings not too far off.

But it's gloomy. I look back, and the only real light comes from the busted open door behind us, but the sun won't travel far inside the dome. It's too gloomy in here for the sun to light our way. It's too quiet. Where is everybody? Both Miranda1 and William1 say it's a busy place, with one thousand children, but it's silent and still. Our Littluns would never be so quiet, and there's only a handful of them. Or there was. I try not to think about that.

Miranda moves into a grove of trees with flowers. It smells sweet, and I whisper to Cranker, "Fruit trees!" My heart pounds, I want to stop and touch the miracle trees, but Miranda1 walks fast, and we run to catch up.

Then there's a sight that just about makes my heart jump out of my mouth. Under a huge tree there's a monster made all of metal and leather, and another, both taller than me by far. The two monsters are locked together by shiny metal hands. They spin around, slow, looking at each other as they spin, spin, spin. There's a high, sharp whine from one of them. I cover my ears.

"What the jigger?" Cranker whispers, standing close beside me. I don't know what the monsters are, but I seen the behavior before. It's like the one-eyed dog holding a FatRat in its skinny jaws.

They mean to harm one another. The two metal monsters clutch each other in a death grip if ever I seen one.

MIRANDA1

I step into the Seed Park. Caliban and Ariel slip from tree to tree ahead of me, silent as shades, much quieter than the two boys behind me. I leave the door and the sunlight and lead us all into Oculum.

"Miranda1," Mann whispers and points ahead of us.

A Mother and a Sentry are locked together beneath the walnut tree. They spin, slowly, each with a metallic hand arched around the heart of the other. A high, metallic whine comes from them, and my own heart skips a beat. My breathing speeds up.

What are this Mother and Sentry doing? And where are the children?

I creep closer and see that the Mother and the Sentry have their eyes locked on one another, as tightly as their metallic arms. I toss a fallen stick near the pair, (I'm shocked that a stick has been allowed to lie untended — where are the Treekeepers to clean it up?), but the Mother and Sentry don't hear me or see me.

"It's Miranda1, returned from Outside!" I call, but they don't turn toward me.

"What's up with them?" Cranker asks. I shrug.

William1's note on his map comes to me: *The Mothers will help us. The Sentries will not.*

"I have no idea. But this should be a bustling market day. There should be children and their Mothers all over the common, all across the main street." I lead the dogs and the boys across the silent Seed Park, then I walk behind the Medicus Hall and onto the main street. There are no children anywhere.

Then I see another Sentry and a Mother outside the Teaching Hall.

They're locked together too, spinning slowly, each with a mechanical hand held deeply into the other's chest. There is the same high, metallic whine.

A sudden chill starts at my neck. I do know what the whine is; I have heard my own Mother make this noise when I climbed the walnut tree at twelve during my coming-of-age rite and almost fell.

The Mother is screaming.

I get a rise of panic.

"They fighting?" Mann asks softly.

"I don't know," I say. "I've never seen this before. Tread quietly." The dogs and the boys help calm me, and I thank William1 again for sending them. We go past the spinning Mother and Sentry, but they don't notice us.

"Where are the children?" Mann whispers as we creep along. I shake my head. We slip across the common and look toward the Oculum Senate, and all three of us stop and stare.

Cranker says, "Festering mercy." He has a colorful way with his words.

The square is full of hundreds of Mothers and Sentries locked together, their hands grasping the heart of the other as they spin. The air vibrates with the metallic whine of screaming Mothers.

It makes my hair prickle, my heart race. The dogs stick close to me, the boys too, and once again I'm thankful I am not alone. It's eerie, and I have no idea what is happening.

The last line of William1's poem comes back to me: *The Mothers shall rise, at the call.*

Can this be connected? I don't see how. What call? Whose call?

We pass the Senate, and I'm afraid to look in, but I must. We creep up the stairs and open the heavy wooden door. The Atrium is full of more spinning Mothers and Sentries, more screaming. The noise is terrifying, amplified in the marble hall.

I can't bear to look at my own Mother, but I make myself peek … and Regulus still lies there dead at the bottom of the great Arm, Mother slumped on top of him. So far, they are the only two casualties that I have seen. Cranker swears softly again. Mann just stares with wide eyes, and I realize they are amazed by the Oculum Arm. It is impressive.

But I have no time to explain. What has happened to the children?

We step out into the square, past the spinning, screaming Mothers and Sentries, and again none of them notice us. We hurry toward the houses, running along the silent streets, but there is no one.

Then, a quick closing of a curtain, a sly, silent click of a front door.

We are being watched. "There's someone over there," Cranker whispers, and I see a child whip behind a building. I almost faint with relief.

They are not destroyed.

I stop running and lead the dogs and the two boys across a street. I stride up the front steps of a house with a red door and "W2" in silver lettering. I bang upon the door.

"WILLIAM2! WILLIAM2! Open the door! I know you're in there! It's me, Miranda1!" The front window curtain flickers, an eye sees me, then the door opens with a quiet *click*.

William2 stands in his front hall. He still wears the armband that says "W1," and he looks at me with deep fear. Terror. William2 is terrified of me. I wave at Cranker and Mann and tell them to keep the dogs back, so they wait on the sidewalk in front of the house. My new friends each grab a dog and stay where they are.

I don't want William2 to be too terrified to talk to me. I take a step toward him in his front hallway.

"Stop! Miranda1, I beg you! Come no closer!"

"William2, what has happened? It's me!"

He comes forward then, which is very brave, because he trembles.

"Are you not … are you not dead, Miranda1? Are you not a Fandom from Outside?" he whispers, his eyes wide. I go forward and grab his arm, and he gasps.

"No, William2. I assure you I'm not dead. Do I look dead to you?" William2 is not a stupid boy, or a coward, and he agrees with me.

"No, Miranda1, clearly you're not dead. But what are you doing here? Who are those boys, and creatures?"

"They are my friends. You can trust them. And the creatures are called dogs. I've been Outside, William2. It's the real world, and we must all go there. But we must hurry!"

He stares at me, shakes his head. "I thought — we thought — you told your Mother to kill Regulus, and now the Sentries and Mothers are locked in battle!"

"I did not tell my Mother to kill Regulus, William2. She did that herself, to give me time to get away and climb the Arm."

He blinks at me. "Why?" he asks. The look on Mother's face as I climbed, on Grannie's face leaning over her sick, the last line of the poem from William1's book … there is only one answer.

"It can only be to help. Perhaps … perhaps it is for love?"

"Love?" he whispers. I nod. *Poor boy*, I think. This is all too strange. Death, then a lie, escape, and now love.

But there's no time; we can discuss it later.

"We do not have much time, William2. Whatever the Mothers and Sentries are doing, it may not last. They may notice us soon. We must hurry and leave. Where are the children?" I ask gently.

He is calmer now. "They are all hiding in their houses." He is about to say something more, but there's a knock at the door and a child's voice.

"William? I have seen Miranda1! Is she there?"

William2 is frozen to the spot, but I rush and open the door. Jake47 stands on the doorstep, and when he sees me, he leaps forward and holds me tight. He looks up at me and whispers, "I knew you would not abandon us." There's a noise outside, and more children gather on the sidewalk, standing close to Cranker and Mann. The dogs patiently allow many small hands to stroke them. Ariel appears to be enjoying the attention, while Caliban is merely resigned.

I take Jake47 by the hand, and William2 follows us out onto his front porch. There are many children gathered now, and when they see me, they cheer. I raise my staff.

"Children of Oculum! It's me, Miranda1! We must hurry and leave Oculum. Gather your belongings! Quickly!" A dozen young voices call to me, and hands grab at mine. I must look very strange with my tall staff, standing in Grannie's boots, with two satchels across my chest and wearing William1's clothes. Not to mention the two strange boys I have with me and the dogs. I must seem like a wayfarer from afar, which is exactly what I am.

More doors open, and suddenly children run toward us from every direction.

"Gather your belongings! Hurry! Meet on the common!" I call again and again. Soon, Mann, Cranker, the dogs, William2, and I lead a growing group of children to every door of Oculum. Children scamper up every step, every front door bangs open, every face sees us and joins the throng. Children rush out of their homes, and every child carries a bulging satchel of clothes and food.

I rush to my old home. I yank open the purple door with "M1" on it and step back into my old life. Cranker and Mann and the dogs run inside with me, and they're amazed.

"This all yours? Just for you?" Mann asks, stilled.

"Yes, everyone in Oculum has a house," I say, running to gather supplies. I saw his home in the courtyard with Grannie. I know where he comes from and where we're all headed. Outside is not like Oculum, but it is the truth, and none of us can stay here.

I run to my bedroom and grab shoes, a frock, another cloak, and put these in my empty satchels. I hastily take all the food I can find from the pantry, more peaches, more apples, more dried fruit and sealed jugs of water, then we all hurry back out to the enormous crowd filling the street.

I call out: "Children of Oculum! Our world is not what we think. There is Outside, and sunshine, and starlight, and we must go there! There are good people like these two boys with me. There are strange, wonderful creatures like these dogs. Go now, knock on every door! But hurry, we do not have much time. The Mothers and the Sentries could wake at any moment!"

The children run to their homes, and Oculum is alive again with children's calls and slamming doors and breathless exchanges.

I am about to hurry the crowd toward the Senate when Mann grabs my arm. He looks up.

"We got a problem," he says quietly. Cranker and I follow his eyes, and there, across the top of Oculum, runs a deep, heavy crack. It spreads upward from William1's broken door and across the peak of our world. The crack stops for a moment. Then starts. Then stops again.

BOOM!

The shock of the noise stops everyone, and every eye looks up. A small piece of glass falls from above the door into the Seed Park, and the youngest children scream. Suddenly, terrified, screaming children come from every direction at a run. William2 runs up with a group of Williams, Mirandas, Henrys, and Samanthas, the twelve- and thirteen-year-old boys and girls, the oldest in Oculum.

"What can we do?" William2 yells over the noise of the children.

I think quickly. "Gather the youngest children in your arms, each of you! We must all go to the Senate ..."

BOOM!

Another piece of the wall falls, far off, and children scream. Mann says, "The whole thing is coming down!"

Then Cranker adds, "That's not the end of it." He points toward the Senate.

I turn to look and gasp. The Mothers and Sentries have all fallen still.

Each metallic face has turned to face us.

The nearest Mother sees me, and all the children gathered around me, with more running my way. The Mother and I stare at each other for a moment, then William1's note and the words from the poem on his map click in my head: *The Mothers shall rise, at the call.*

If ever we needed our Mother's to rise, it's now.

"MOTHERS! IT'S MIRANDA1! HELP US! PROTECT US!" I shout with everything I have. The nearest Mother doesn't hesitate. With a shriek, the Mother drives her metallic hand deep into the chest of the Sentry before her. With a vicious yank, she rips out its heart.

The Sentry slumps forward, dead. The other Mothers watch for a moment, then with a horrifying shriek, all the Mothers fall upon the Sentries.

"RUN!" I shout, and frightened children race toward me in waves.

BOOM!

Another small piece of the wall falls at the edge of Oculum. Cranker, Mann, and the dogs run across the square, dodging Mothers and Sentries, and the rest of us stream behind them. Metallic arms whip past us, crash into metallic chests, wrench out metallic hearts. The sound of shrieking metal and screaming Mothers deafens the wails of the children. I see a Mother fall, her heart crushed in the hands of the Sentry that has just killed her. The Sentry turns toward us, but another Mother falls upon it and tears out its heart. And again and again, all around us, the Mothers and Sentries rip and tear, pull and crush, scream and whir.

We must make it to the Senate!

The Williams and Mirandas rush past me, each carrying small Andrews and Annas. The Henrys and Samanthas all run with a young child by the hand or carry them. The rest of the children come too, their satchels bulging with food and water.

"INTO THE SENATE!" I yell. The children of Oculum follow behind me, Cranker and Mann and the dogs at our head, and we all rush into the Atrium, past more battling Mothers and Sentries. Mechanical arms flail viciously as we duck and dodge at a run. There is one last thing we must do before we leave our crumbling world.

BOOM! BOOM!

"Follow me!" I shout. We run toward the Seed Vault, and the children, all of us suddenly know what must be done. With a shock of recognition, I see that it has been my destiny all my life to lead the children of Oculum and our precious cargo in this moment.

The world Outside has been waiting for us, all along.

WILLIAM1

Grannie says we'll go to her brother's house, get men and women to help, and find a way back into Oculum. So that is what we will do. I look behind us constantly for any sign of Cranker, Mann, and Miranda1, but all is quiet. More carts go past us. There are adults, grown people, even old people, animals, and huge machines, and much more here. It's not like Oculum. There's the sky above, and the earth beneath, and all these people on the road and living in the ruined city are free to move and go as they please.

It is not as beautiful as Oculum, perhaps, but it is the real world. I know that now.

We travel the road in the cart pulled by the horses. I talk to the three children in the cart behind me, and they are polite but they all seem in awe of me.

Grannie is growing more curious about my domed world, too, although the questions are few and far between, and are most often about the youngest children and who takes care of them.

"You got Mothers in there?" she asks, surprised, when I tell her. I nod. I hold the book the thieves ruined,

For the Children of Oculum, on my lap.

"Yes, but they're not like you or me. They're machines, I know that now. But clever machines. The book explained it all. They were made by the people who left us there long ago. You call them Olden Begones. A Mother's job is to raise her child, but she must also protect her child from the Sentries when the first of us talks of love. Or when the first of us escapes Oculum through a hidden door." Grannie looks over at me, the reins loose in her hand as the cart rattles along.

"That be you, then? You the first out the door?"

"Yes, and then Miranda1, but I can't imagine how she did it." I really can't. The door must have been guarded by the Sentries after I walked through it. How did she manage to get near it?

"The book says that once a child of Oculum talks of love, then the Mothers must prepare for us to leave. Both of these things seem to be inevitable, love and leaving, at least to the writers of the book."

"Well, love and leaving is part of growing up," Grannie says.

I nod. "Yes, Grannie, but none of us has grown up, at least not until now." I think about that for a moment. Miranda1 and I have the job of being the oldest, being the first in everything.

"But the book says something else. When the first child leaves, the Sentries will try to stop everyone else from leaving, since their only purpose is to keep Oculum safe. And to a Sentry, keeping Oculum safe means keeping everyone inside the dome. No one can leave."

Grannie strokes her chin, thinking. "Seems like contraries. The Mothers raise healthy children to leave Oculum, as is only natural, but these Sentries protect Oculum by keeping all the children safe inside? Seems like a good reason for a fight."

I raise my eyebrows. She's wise, Grannie. And she's right. The Mothers and the Sentries are opposites: Mothers protect the children, and Sentries protect Oculum. But the children grow up, and change must come. The book didn't mention a fight between Mothers and Sentries, but for the thousandth time, I worry about what's happening back in my domed world. It's more important than ever for me to find Miranda1 and then for us to get back there.

Grannie has given me a sheet of paper, which is rare, she tells me. I thank her, and I use my ink pot and feather quill to write down what I can remember from the ruined book. It had only a dozen pages in a beautiful hand before the thieves ruined it, so it's not that hard. I've written down what I can remember about a Mother's purpose and a Sentry's purpose. I have copied the poem about the door. The last three lines run in my head ...

Be the brave ones,
Then pass beyond it,
The Mothers shall rise, at the call.

I write as the cart rolls along, hour after hour, and we stop for midday meal. I hand Grannie my last peach, and she finally takes it from me, and smells it, and then puts it in her apron pocket.

"It's too precious," she says, but she smiles. Today, though, I think she will taste it.

The sun beats down. Lisle sleeps, the little boys sleep, and I keep writing upon my paper. Then ... I lift my head.

There is a sound like a wave coming toward us.

"What's that?" I say, peering down the road. We're near the top of a hill. Grannie stops the cart and listens. The noise gets louder; it's almost a roar. It's louder again, coming our way. I strain my ears, and it's the sound of feet. And talking. A lot of people, talking.

Our cart is almost at the top of a hill, but we can't see what's beyond the rise.

Grannie stands up in the front of the cart and shields her eyes from the sun. She looks surprised, then worried.

"What the heck? William, you're taller. Stand up, have a look." I lean one hand on Grannie's shoulder and shakily stand in the front the cart. I can just see over the lip of the hill.

A black dog and a huge gray dog run over the hill and see us, then stop.

"They were with Cranker and Mann!" I shout.

Then I see them. My heart almost leaps out of my chest. Over the hill behind the dogs, flows a river of children of all colors. There are one thousand children, rippling down the road, behind two boys and a girl leading them. I strain and see them clearly. It's Mann and Cranker at their head!

And Miranda1 with a staff, holding a child's hand!

Grannie tries to stop me, but I grab my crutch and leap from the cart. I limp as fast as I can toward the mighty girl who has somehow led the children of Oculum to their freedom, and her dearest of hearts back to me.

MANNFRED

William1 comes at a run, pretty fast too for a boy with a limp.

He seems to have forgot about his ankle. He waves, and Miranda1 sees him then drops hands with a child and tears off. The two catch each other in the road, and there's a lot of hugging, and laughing, and then more hugging again.

Cranker and me walk up to Grannie, and we say hello. But she's only got eyes for one thing: the river of children we brought her. Children, Littluns of every size and age imaginable, just keep coming over that hill. They all got leather bags, and some of the older ones carry small green trees in their arms or sticking out of their satchels. Some of the bigger boys and girls have the littlest children on their shoulders. I carried a fair share of Littluns myself today.

Grannie just stares. Then she gets down out of the cart and comes over to Miranda1. "What you done here, girl?"

"I have brought the children of Oculum, Grannie," she says simply.

"But Miranda, how?" William1 asks.

"Oh, it's too much to tell," she says wearily. "I climbed the Arm and then wandered in the rubble looking for you, then Mann and Cranker found me," she says. William looks at her, astonished.

"You climbed the *Arm*?" He shakes his head. "But how did you get back in to get the children? Then how did you get past the Sentries to get *out*?"

I can see Miranda is too tired to answer him, so I pipe up. "Cranker and me busted the door open with a rock and a piece of metal a few days ago, although we didn't know it 'til we went back. Made a mess of the dome, too, it's falling to pieces."

I see a light turn on in William's head. "You! You lost the Map of Oculum!" he whispers, and Miranda1 nods. Cranker reaches into his bag and pulls out the map, a little crumpled but still in one piece. William takes it but barely looks at it.

"How did you all escape? The Sentries were designed to keep you there."

"We almost didn't get past them," I say. "We had to run, the Mothers took care of the Sentries."

William just looks at him. "A battle then?" he says, and Cranker and me nod.

"Who won?" William1 asks, and we both shrug. "It was still happening when we left through the busted door," I say. "We made it, though," Cranker adds, "so I'd say the Mothers done their best." It must seem unreal to William1. It's still impossible to me, those Mothers chasing the Sentries and ripping out all those hearts. They were still at it by the time we gathered all the seeds and trees, then ran to the door and back out into the sunlight.

"'Course your mothers fought for you. That's no surprise," Grannie says. She looks like someone who discovered a fountain of sweet water. She walks among the children, placing her hands on their heads, saying hello, cuddling the littlest and asking their names, telling them hers. She's already got a wave of the smallest ones around her, following her close like they don't want to take their eyes off her.

Miranda1 speaks to Grannie. "We need shelter, homes, someone to guide us. This is a strange world, nothing like the one we've known before." And she and Grannie walk among the children and get to talking. The older children hold the little ones on their back or in their arms, but we're all exhausted. I want to sit down.

I'm still shy with all the children from Oculum, even though I helped rescue them, and I been walking among them for hours. The boys are pleasant, the girls too, but there's a lot of them now in the road, all staring at the horses. They never seen horses, and they ask to touch them. Nancy and Nellie aren't so sure about all these children, though, so I tell them to come one at a time and let them feel a horse's soft nose for the first time.

Soon the Williams and the Mirandas organize all the

children to sit in the grass beside the road and eat.

Every single child brings out a piece of fruit. Peaches, apples, and pears. Dried cherries. It's like some kind of dream I always had, watching an army of children eating fruit in the field on a beautiful spring day. Our three Littluns stare from the cart like they been struck dumb, so I ask a child if I can have three dried cherries, and I take them to the cart. The Littluns get big eyes, and quiet, when they pop the fruit in their mouths.

"Keep the seeds!" Miranda1 tells everyone. "We'll need them when we reach our new home. Put them beside your seed packets," she says, holding up a small sack.

"Seed packets?" William1 asks.

"Yes, from the Seed Vault in the Senate, we each took a packet of seeds from every drawer, all one thousand of them," she says, then yawns.

And I laugh. I just start to laugh, and Cranker asks what's wrong, and I split my sides. I sweep an arm out over the field of children, and their fruit and seeds and tree cuttings, and I feel like I could bust.

What can I say? Cranker, there's a whole field of new Littluns, a whole field of lost seeds. And it's our luck to make friends with them, take care of them, and grow all the food and peach trees we could ever want. I also happen to know that two of the older children carry a sturdy new kind of bees meant for this world, a hive each in a soft sack, all ready to swarm and live.

It seems impossible.

After we all eat, Grannie steps into the cart, and William1 and Miranda1 join her. Then she sets the horses off down the road, and all of us walk slow behind her. We're going to her brother's house, to his houses and lands, and he's going to be mighty surprised when we get there.

After a while, a man on a horse comes by and looks amazed at all the children, then he talks to Grannie for a bit, tips his hat, and rides off hasty. A little while later, another man and a woman ride up, and talk to Grannie, then they ride away fast. Sometime later another man rides up and tells Grannie something and rides away. Grannie calls me over.

"We're the talk of the City," she grins.

"'Course we are, Grannie. Have you noticed all the children walking behind the cart? Have you forgot that they got peaches, and pears, and apples? And their pockets and satchels are full of seeds and cutting from fruit trees, all of them? Not to mention two hives of bees?"

She spies me out of one eye and says, "The Shiny Man is coming tomorrow. And Jonatan Briar, to talk to William1 and Miranda1. In fact, we got worlds of people coming to talk to us. My brother is going to be some-thing surprised." I never seen Grannie look so happy.

"Good people?" I ask. I think about that tall man at the gates with Grannie's gun, and his guards who took

Grannie's goat and hen and more besides, and the shaved-head boy and his gang of thieves. Not everyone will be so happy to see us, maybe. I look over at Miranda1, William1 sitting beside her in the cart, and the two dogs trotting along beside. Good people or bad people coming to speak to them, no one is going to push those two around.

Grannie shrugs. "I don't know, but these children here has a lot to tell them. Here, take Lisle." Grannie unties the blue sling, I slide it over my shoulder, and Lisle settles into my arm. She's sleeping and sucking on the soother I made her.

I fall back into the crowd and strike up a chat with a girl named Miranda32, who's fascinated with Lisle. I discover that children don't leave what's called a *nursery* in her world until they're four, so they seen a baby before through glass, but never up close. Once she tells the others, I got a lot of children coming close to peek at Lisle, stroke her soft cheek, and she just sleeps through all of it.

Hours we walk along the main road across the City, but it's easy walking. All the piles of houses are cleared and away from us. I never talked to so many people in my life. I never laughed so hard, I never asked so many questions, I never struggled so hard to explain what my life's been like up to now.

Sometime, just before dark, one of the boys about my age says, "Look!"

We all look back the way we come. Way off in the distance, a whole day's walk behind us, we see the side of the dome start to fall in on itself. Then the whole thing collapses and a mighty cloud of dust blows up into the sky. A second later we hear the distant rumble as the great glass Oculum City Dome tumbles down.

It was going to happen; I'm just glad it didn't crash onto our heads during our escape. The children from that place watch, and a few sigh a little, all their Mothers and homes must be gone now. But no one's too upset. They were nothing but prisoners in a glass world, and now they know it.

And as far as I can tell, they like it out here in the rubble and the rocks.

Cranker comes up to me as we stop for the night and says, "Figure your rock and my metal piece brought down that dome, Mann?" I stretch into my sleeping roll on the grass beside the road, surrounded by one thousand sleepy Littluns, and look up at the stars.

"Seems impossible, but maybe. We started a little crack that brought down the door. Could be it grew and broke the whole thing. It's old, like all the other buildings around. Maybe it couldn't stand being broke? But who'd believe it? I know one thing. When I see Jonatan Briar tomorrow, I got a story for him. And William1 has his map, for the library on Briar's island, and a few books to write for him, too."

Cranker laughs. "How long you figure it'll take us to

grow a peach tree?" he asks a while later.

I open an eye, but I'm too tired to answer. I fall asleep, dreaming of something Miranda1 told me was called orchards, and the scent and beauty of apple blossoms and pear blossoms and cherry trees.

I can't wait to get farming when we get to Grannie's brother's house.

It'll take a long time, my whole life and then some, but I got only one wish: one day, when I'm a man, me and my friends, my family, everybody there is, will pick peaches big as barrels, sweet as honey, from trees tall as the sky.

ACKNOWLEDGEMENTS

I don't often write an acknowledgement page, so thank you to publisher Barry Jowett at DCB for this one! And thank you to both Barry and Marc Côté, publisher of Cormorant Books, for welcoming me aboard. I'm so honoured to have my middle-grade dystopia in their talented hands.

This book began as a weird, vivid dream, in which mechanical arms tucked a human child into bed. I'm not sure whose arms they were (or whose child), but I did take inspiration for the Mothers in this story from parenting my own children, Sarah and Ben. Thank you to them for our bedtime ritual which always ended with a little extra tucking before the lights went out.

I'd like to acknowledge that the character of Grannie in this story is inspired by the heroic feats of grandmothers the world over, raising the next generation of children orphaned by AIDS, war, addiction or in the case of this book, the end of the world. I've also taken much inspiration from my lifelong friend Sarah, to whom this book is dedicated, who has fostered, adopted and supported many, many children over the years, all who needed loving arms.

Many thanks to the early readers of this book, Doris Montanera, Iris Wilde, and Rebecca Upjohn, who were so willing and so right. Another enormous thank you to friend and children's author Monica Kulling, who not only read the book in its early stages, but who was a tireless champion of both it and me.

I must thank my steadfast editor too, Allister Thompson, who has worked with me through eleven books now, including this one. I can't do what he does, nor can I imagine doing what I do without his expert help. And here's a huge, grateful "WOW" to Emma Dolan, the illustrator of the beautiful cover of this book. The image of Mother of Miranda1 is exactly as I had imagined her, somehow. Thank you, Emma.

My influences for this dystopia come from my own childhood favourite books, like John Christopher's *White Mountains Trilogy*, which was the first dystopia I ever read at age ten, and John Wyndham's *The Chrysalids* a few years later. Authors I revisited while writing this book were Lois Lowry, Cormac McCarthy, PD James, Margaret Atwood, Monica Hughes, Ursula K Le Guin, George Orwell, Ray Bradbury and others. Thanks all for the inspiration and the vision!

And here's my chance to thank all those booksellers, educators, and librarians who care deeply about children's books, who get the right book to the right child, and seed the next generation with readers and storytellers. You're all superheroes to me, now and when I was the child seeking the right book. Thank you to parents, grandparents and caregivers who read to their children, too, and develop in them an early curiosity and a lifelong love of reading. We need readers and story-tellers, now and always.

Finally a thought for readers of this book. While I hope no one ever inherits a world like *Oculum*, (who wants to live in a world without peaches?), I do hope that what-ever may come, kindness and community will prevail as it does for Miranda and Mann in this story.

The very last thank you is for Paul, my partner of 35 years, who brings me lunch long after I forget, and who has never failed in all those years to keep the lights on!

Philippa Dowding
February 2018

Photo by: Andrea Gutsche

Philippa Dowding has won many magazine awards and has had poetry and short fiction published in journals across Canada. Her children's books have been nominated for numerous literary awards in Canada, in the U.S., and Europe, including the SYRCA Diamond Willow, OLA Silver Birch Express, OLA Red Maple, and Hackmatack awards. In 2017, she won the OLA Silver Birch Express Honour Book Award for *Myles and the Monster Outside*.